Flesh Evidence

Malcolm Hollingdrake

Book Three in the Harrogate Crime Series

Second Edition

First published in 2016

ISBN: 978-1-9160715-2-0

Praise for Malcolm Hollingdrake

Flesh Evidence is the third book in the DCI Cyril Bennett series and boy! what a book. It can easily be read as a stand-alone but as it's a great series would recommend reading them all.

I really have to take my hat off to the author for this brilliant story line. It literally grabbed me by the collar and sent me hurdling full speed through the book.

Sarah Hardy - By the letter Book Reviews

Fantastic book great addition to the DCI Bennett series I couldn't put this book down. Having lived in and around Harrogate area I could imagine the area that this is set. Also the descriptive writing is amazing. I have enjoyed this book and I can say that Malcolm Hollingdrake is now one of my favourite authors.

Martin Cochrane

Wow! I must say a well-deserved five stars. I was seriously impressed. If the cover doesn't grab your attention then this one of a kind story will.

Gemma Gaskarth – Between the pages book club

It's heart breaking and so expertly written, with an ingenious plot twist.

Caroline Vincent- Bits about Books

This is the third novel in Malcolm Hollingdrake's series and I will be damned if you can find anything like these stories because, oh man are they original.

Susan Hampson – Books from Dawn Till Dusk

Also by

Malcolm Hollingdrake

Bridging the Gulf

Shadows from the Past
Short Stories for Short Journeys

The Harrogate Crime Series

Only the Dead

Hell's Gate

Flesh Evidence

Game Point

Dying Art

Crossed Out

The Third Breath

Treble Clef

ı know I can't release you, not yet anyway, you're

ɔved hand removed a rolling tear from the youth's
blood-tinged tongue licked it from the blue latex
ıing off the music.
e for you to rest and calm down."
light went off and the world was again black and

I dedicate this book to two fine fellows

William Hollingdrake and William Clark

Without whom we would be nobody.

Prologue

7th August 1976

The warmth of the long summer showed no sign of abating. The south-facing windows of the hospital trapped more and more of the day's incessant heat; the waiting room seemed to grow increasingly claustrophobic as the air grew thick, warm and sticky, emphasising the indelible hospital aroma. Pamphlets full of advice for young parents hung as listlessly as the air from discoloured cork lined walls, each held at one corner by a solitary drawing pin of varying colours. Ian Dixon let his eyes follow them round the room. He counted the different coloured pins to alleviate his anxiety. It was then he heard his name being called, disturbing the silence. Butterflies shot through his stomach.

"You have a son, Mr Dixon. Congratulations!"

His heart raced as he moved towards the delivery room. There, cradled in Jose's arms was his first born, a son, Samuel.

Chapter One

The keen edge of the blade
stretched flesh, squeezing va
beads of blood which sat
surface. Some gorged and
bursting and running round th
now healing, criss-crossed n
taped lips and the twitching
music playing in the backgro
macabre pantomime.

It was always their e
old, their eyes told the true
deeply within those dark pc
Those same crying eyes foll
tongue traced the sliced fles
filled beads one by one. T
coming together, savouring t
one person in the room it wa

"You're not sweet e
it will take another week, ma
are we? And the only thin
children!"

A smile moved acros
father's advice you know ar
I'm sure you might think onl
away from the world."

Tears continued to
and so alive, as the throb c
his sliced arm.

"Yo
not ready."

A g
cheek. The
before swit

"Ti

The
silent.

Chapter Two

Late July 2015

The shrill screams carried by the wind managed to infiltrate the music streamed to Tony's ears from his phone. He paused, removing his left earphone to listen. It was much clearer and more high-pitched above the squeezed sounds he felt vibrate in his closed hand. He smiled to himself as the excitement grew within him, he had been looking forward to this for such a long time. Returning the earphone, he thrust his hand deeply into his pocket.

His fingers began to fumble the coins for the fifth time. He ran them through his fingers one at a time like an umpire counting off the balls in an over. There were definitely eight or was it nine? He checked again. Once satisfied he slipped his hand into his back pocket and removed the folded notes. Two fives and four tens; he returned them and tapped the outer pocket still able to feel the outline. He smiled to himself partly in pleasure; he felt no guilt. If his dad ever discovered that he had stolen money from anywhere, let alone the house there would be hell to pay, but he was smarter than that. He had learned to be patient, to choose the correct moment. He only took money when he considered it to be safe, the odd coin here and there, but more on the occasions when his parents returned from a night out. It was easy to get up early and slip the odd fiver away when it was left crunched in the bowl in the kitchen along with car keys and the odd tissue. There had been a couple of times when his father, not suffering from a hangover, had questioned whether his mother had taken any money, but that was as close to suspicion as it got. Nothing was ever pursued, his father responded with a quick raise of the shoulders and a quizzical look. It was then Tony would ask for a pound for this or that and predictably he would succeed. A double victory!

The Stray Fair was the main reason for the deception; well you could not go to a fair with only a few quid, some rides alone were more than his weekly spending money.

The grass was still damp from the afternoon's rain. Tony's shoes were already soaked through from the kick about earlier. When he removed his earphones, he could hear and see the Fair, the loud music collided with more loud music as each ride operator tried to outdo the other. The myriad flashing coloured lights along with the chorus of intermittent screams from excited girls, produced a Siren's welcome against the darkening day. Tony's heart fluttered with excitement. He replaced his earphones and stared, the noise from the Fair now drowned out by the shrill music bombarding his ears.

"Tooonnneee!" Colin's voice sounded like a football fan chanting his favourite team's name, emphasising the last vowel for what seemed like an age.

On the fourth call Tony heard it and turned. Colin and Mark ran towards him, arms outstretched like aeroplanes coming in for attack.

"You're bloody late! You said the war memorial." Tony looked at his phone. "Half an hour ago!" He flicked off the music.

"And you're bloody deaf… da,da,da,da… bandits from 7'oclock."

Tony removed his earphones and wrapped them round his mobile. "Funny, I don't think."

"Mark couldn't get money from his dad until he'd washed up and taken the dog out. It's like the Gestapo at his house. Any road, we're here, we've money to burn and there's fun to be had. Dodgems, waltzer and then maybe we should try the killer ride *2xtreme*." He emphasised the word and pulled a terrified expression as if it were totally evil. The boys laughed more at the gurned face than the thought of the ride as they began to run towards the Fair.

It was busy. They headed straight for the waltzer, the ride's flashing lights, blasting music and screaming girls proving an aphrodisiac to the three lads. It was better than they had expected and they rode it twice.

"Bloody Hell it's fast! I've got a feeling I might be losing my tea sometime tonight!" screamed Tony, struggling to make himself heard. The cars were spun eagerly by the staff who always seemed to pick the ones containing the prettiest girls.

"Some fighter pilot you'll make, you tart. You can go on your own after the next ride. These are my best jeans and I don't want you pebble-dashing them with mashed up beans on toast."

They laughed even more.

***

Tony was right. At about ten o'clock, after a final fling on a carrousel, he bought a hot dog, drank the complimentary sweet fizzy drink and within minutes threw up into a convenient waste bin.

"Jesus Colin, did you see the colour of that? It was like blancmange."

"I'm done!" Tony wiped his mouth with the back of his hand. "I feel like shit. Anyway, I have to be in by eleven. Coming?"

"You're grey boy, really like a ghost. I told you not to eat the crap they produce at these places. Probably got some strange plague. No, one more ride for us. Remember Tony, some guys are tougher than the rest." They started laughing and slapped him on the back.

Tony pushed in the two earpieces and turned on his phone's music, adjusting the volume to near maximum, blotting out the surrounding sounds. He started to walk away from the Fair. The sudden feeling of nausea swept through his stomach and the stinging acidic taste hit the back of his throat. He felt a prickly heat flush through his body and then suddenly felt cold. He kneeled by some bushes surrounding a copse of trees bordering the edge of The Stray. Remnants of the hot dog mixed with a pink froth exploded from his lips as the sweat formed on his forehead. The music still flooded his hearing.

The gloved hand touching Tony's head was gentle at first, almost caressing, definitely reassuring. It remained as Tony saw another hand offering a pack of tissues and then a bottle of water.

"This'll help you. You look terrible." The voice was low and comforting.

Tony turned and saw the friendly lips move as if in slow motion but he did not hear the words. He smiled, confused by the sudden illness and took the offerings.

"You need some help. Come."

***

It was the absolute fear in Tony's eyes, the look of uncertainty, hopelessness and incomprehensible bewilderment, the near surrender that brought the greatest thrill. It was like a shot of pure adrenalin. Even in the cold and dark of the container you could still see it and feel it. The same glass jar was placed into Tony's left hand, a plastic spoon protruding from the lip.

"Eat, Tony!"

That was all the person said. Those same lips moved, seemingly gentle and strangely caring. Tony's stomach turned as he fought back the nausea of fear. A gloved hand ruffled his hair. This time there was no reassurance.

"If you scream, you know what the result will be, but after this week together, we're getting to know each other better, we understand what we like don't we, Tony?"

Tony could see the gleam of the knife. His eyes looked at the lines on his arms and in places he noticed the remnants of dried blood smearing his white skin. The blade slit the grey gaffer tape holding his bound right wrist and elbow to the arm of the commode.

"Eat whilst I take away your mess."

The galvanised bucket was lifted from the wooden space beneath Tony's seat; the faeces produced a strange, almost sweet smell as the container was brought out into the open.

"We're nearly there."

Tony could hear the deep inhalation and the rattle of the bucket's handle.

"Five minutes to eat, no longer."

Tony moved his free arm, grabbed at the spoon and ate. The jar's contents were the same as yesterday and the day before that but it was food and this was all he would get until the following day.

Chapter Three

Late August 2015

The whiteboards surrounding the incident room were full of images; Tony Thompson, wearing jeans, Tony Thompson wearing his school uniform, his football strip, his Air Cadet uniform. They helped form a clear picture of the youth, his safe return being their immediate goal. There were also the photographs of his parents, relatives and friends, all annotated, whilst Scene of Crime images filled another board alongside maps of Oatlands' Stray. The files had grown over the three weeks since his disappearance but there was nothing, it was as if he had been swallowed up, gone.

DCI Cyril Bennett had been asked to support the investigation team but it was with a clear understanding that it was purely support. His Governor's words still played in his head. "Sensitive interaction, Cyril. No bulls, no broken china!"

The missing youth seemed to have simply vanished. CCTV footage showed nothing. Forensics had their hands tied as there was no real crime scene, unless you counted the whole area that comprised The Stray Fair site. The surrounding area had been submitted to a fingertip search and specialist dogs had been brought in. They had found the three areas of vomit, two matching Tony's DNA. The results had shown that the contents contained syrup of Ipecac, a drug used to induce vomiting. It was strong enough evidence to suggest Tony's abduction.

Cyril flipped through the files, his rimless reading glasses perched on the end of his nose. There had been the usual false alarms from a nationwide media request for information. Three people had admitted to the abduction and murder, two others had purported to be the missing child whilst two offers of help from people who could telepathically determine where the youth would be if they were given an item of his clothing, had been politely rejected.

"And to think these people breathe the same air as us, Owen. Jesus!" Cyril tossed the file onto his desk and leaned back. "The sad thing is that each and every one of these reports had to be investigated... just in case."

"I sometimes wonder if it's not worth giving psychics a chance, you know, a piece of clothing and letting them follow their instinct," Owen stated with a degree of naïve enthusiasm.

"And what if one of these attention-seeking visionaries is a journalist and writes that the North Yorkshire Police are so desperate, so inefficient that they have to resort to quackery. I can read the headline now, Owen, *North Yorkshire Police Force couldn't find its own arse with its hand in its back pocket!* So the answer to your question is a simple, no! What do we know about the drug found in the sample?"

Owen picked up the file before placing it in front of Cyril. "It was only a suggestion, sir, as from where I'm sitting, nobody else seems to hold any answers."

Cyril read aloud. "Made from one fourteenth of an alcoholic extract of the root and rhizomes of Ipecac root..." he then mumbled as he read... "Quick first aid use at home for accidental poisonings... used by individuals with bulimia nervosa... Our lad wasn't weight conscious was he, Owen?"

"No, sir, sports mad, built a bit like a whippet."

"Designed then to induce vomiting. Check with the parents re his eating habits." Cyril paused. He had always had an aversion to bodily fluids, particularly when not his own and he definitely had a phobia about vomit. You could almost see him shudder at the thought. "Says that it's been discontinued. Global production was stopped in 2010."

Cyril raised an eyebrow and closed the file. There was a long pause.

Owen returned. "Ate like a horse parents have said. There's no medication in the house other than general stuff and that's locked away." Owen added the piece of paper to the file.

"Let's go through national missing persons again, narrowing it down to sex, age and similarities to the missing lad... let's say over the last five years. Work through POLKA, (Police Online Knowledge Area) there should be more links with external agencies."

Owen typed in the details and awaited the results.

"With those parameters..." Owen paused, putting his tongue between his teeth as he scrolled down the screen. "We have two at the moment, a Joseph Fairclough and a Jason Townsend, missing August, 2011 and December, 2013, but others might follow. They're now both cold cases. Joseph was out visiting a friend in..." Owen paused collecting his thoughts. "Knutsford?"

"It's in Cheshire, Owen. And Jason?"

"Late night shopping in Liverpool."

"All three were in the north of England. Any fairs around Knutsford at the time?" It was as if Cyril were thinking out loud. "I suppose there was nothing like that in Liverpool unless there were a few attractions set up to keep kids amused whilst parents were trawling the shops. Please check."

***

Tony lay on the bed, a single LED bulb hung from a wire suspended from the rusting, blue steel roof. Condensation had marked the ribs that ran widthways across the old container, causing the paint to flake. A spoon gently pushed the food into the boy's mouth whilst the other hand supported his limp neck. Death was not that far away. His semi-naked body seemed to have shrunk, his skin taut across his ribs. Tony neither needed taping nor locking up, his body was beginning to fade.

He had done well. Three weeks seemed a long time. At first he had refused the food but as the days went on he was only too happy to co-operate, you might even say he was clearly eager. Two days should see the light in his eyes extinguish and then the work could begin. The gloved hand lowered Tony's head onto the soiled pillow. There was now more of a chill in the air. The same hand lifted the piece of chalk and carefully marked another tally on the steel wall. The now silent, moving lips of the captor counted the days.

"We're close, my young friend, very close. Then for you it has ended but for us the game will truly begin."

***

Detective Sergeant David Owen carried two coffees into Cyril's office, one in a mug that Cyril suggested bore more stains than a neglected public urinal and the other in a bone china cup and saucer. A sheaf of papers was wedged between his teeth.

"Have you any idea as to the number of soiled hands that have held those papers, Owen?"

David Owen had always been known as Owen since Police College as there were a number of students named David on the course. Many colleagues now assumed it to be his Christian name.

Owen removed the offending papers and smiled, moving his lips as if ascertaining the answer from the taste. He lifted his shoulders. "I'm getting a touch of sweat maturing into a slight sense on the palate of urine... no, that might be the fried bread I had for breakfast." He smiled at his boss. "You've got to eat some dirt every day to enhance the immune system. That's what my grandmother always said."

"Right!" Cyril looked at Owen's huge frame and thought that she might have been right. They had now worked together for at least five years and although they were like chalk and cheese, they made a formidable team. Owen, in Cyril's mind, was as keen as mustard and a bloody good copper, even though he always looked as though he had entered through a hedge backwards and not through the office door.

"We have a record of a fair not far from Knutsford but it was the week prior to Joseph Fairclough's disappearance. We have a large Ferris Wheel and a few carrousel rides at *Liverpool One*, a large shopping centre that was opened in 2008. Busy at that time of the year, very busy."

"So we have a connection with some sort of fair for every missing youngster. Surely the connection was made during the initial investigation on each occasion?"

Owen nodded.

"And nothing?"

Owen shook his head.

Cyril cupped his hands and looked across at Owen. His focus was aimed at small drops of coffee that fell from Owen's mug onto his soiled tie. He tapped the desk. Owen looked down and noticed the coffee. Lifting his tie he sucked it, totally unaware of Cyril's disgusted expression.

"I want all the reports regarding these fairs and I want them by tomorrow. I also want the names of any known paedophiles from all the areas mentioned."

Cyril checked his watch, lifted it to his ear then shook it before checking it again. "I've an appointment with a Black Sheep in fifteen minutes. Let's say that she's an alcoholic extract of hops with a bit of yeast and water... could if you're not careful make you sick!" He grinned. "Want to meet her?"

"Love to." Owen could always murder a pint on a Friday.

Chapter Four

Late August 2015

Donna Mather had seen enough of the school summer holidays and even though the sun was shining and a laughing throng of people surrounded her, the thought of another two weeks of the kids at home dampened her mood. All she really wanted to do was curl up and weep. As a child she had looked forward to the long summer holidays with eagerness, not that she spent much time in school in her teenage years; given half a chance she would find any opportunity to abscond. Roaming the shopping precinct had held greater attractions but now she had kids it was all so very different. Time at home brought out their worst, they were always under her feet, always demanding this or that, squabbling over the most trivial things. It brought her to the end of her limited patience.

Donna looked at the six-year-old pulling her towards the trestle table that looked precariously full of home-made cakes. Tears crawled in her eyes, a crusty cry constantly hung in her small, whinging throat, matching the congealed snot that seemed a permanent feature beneath her right nostril. Donna had decided that she no longer hated the long summer holiday; at this moment in her young life she found that she loathed this compulsory time together. Infanticide had crossed her mind on more than one occasion but then she felt weak and hated herself even more for considering it.

She grumbled under her breath as the tug-of-war with the little one continued. Where Kylie, her eight-year-old was God only knew. Donna just wanted to join in with the younger child and scream her frustration at the top of her voice, cry real tears and if possible, run... run as far away from this miserable life that she suddenly found claustrophobic and unbearable.

"Mum, mum!" Donna felt Kylie tug on her free arm. "Look what I've been given. He said he'd made it... its honey from bees and it's all mine!"

"Who gave you it?"

"A nice man. He said if I gave him a kiss like the bees kiss flowers he'd give me a present. He gave me this."

Donna frowned quizzically and looked back in the direction from which she thought her daughter had come. Her heart leapt as Adele's scream diminished. Her intense stare appeared to mute all her others senses. The area was full of people mingling at stalls. Donna's eyes moved through the crowds looking at the men, focusing on each face. She had no idea for what she was searching, maybe someone looking in her direction, maybe a man carrying jars, but nobody stood out.

"What have I told you about strangers?" Donna's voice was raised and a number of people turned disapprovingly in her direction. They saw her slap the child before grabbing the jar. The child crashed to the floor adding another scream to the mother-child conversation. The younger one stopped pulling and crying before moving close to her mother's legs. She stared at her sister.

"It's mine, he gave it to me."

Donna bent down whispering in her ear, "Wait till your stepdad hears what you've done, young lady. You'll need more than honey to sweeten his temper."

Kylie stopped screaming and turned her gaze towards her mum. She moved her head from side to side, her eyes pleading.

"Stop this tantrum and promise to share this." She waved the honey jar as if she were offering a white flag with which to surrender. "Share it with your sister and we'll say nothing else about it."

Kylie slowly got up. She nodded whilst holding out her hand for the jar.

"Sorry!" she whispered.

***

Kylie and Adele sat at the kitchen table.

"We can all have some of my honey, even dad," Kylie announced as she looked at her mum, a thin guilty smile on her small lips, in the hope that the promise would be kept.

The jar sat in front of Donna who read the hand-written label, *Bees' Kiss Yorkshire Honey*. She turned the jar and focused on the amber contents. There seemed to be something written on the reverse of the label. She looked more closely. There was something in the jar. She had seen honeycombs in jars of honey before but this was not a comb. Twisting the lid, she peered through the surface.

"Can we put our fingers in?" Kylie asked as she pretended to lick her finger in anticipation.

Donna leaned towards the children proffering the jar. Each child put in a finger and immediately popped its sticky amber contents into her mouth. For the first time in what seemed an age Donna heard the girls laugh together. She too put her finger into the jar and laughed in concert.

"Mummy, this honey is so sweet and yummy." They both laughed out loud. "It's yummy mummy, yummy mummy."

"What's going on in here?" Paul swayed into the kitchen.

The laughter stopped as quickly as it had started as the children looked down at the table.

"We all think this honey is mummy yummy honey, don't we girls?" Donna chuckled offering Paul the jar.

They cautiously laughed again watching for clues in their father's expression.

He leaned over and pushed his finger into the jar before licking it.

"Mummy… that's yummy honey!" His demeanour surprised the girls.

They all laughed. Donna looked on, she so wanted to capture the moment, a real family enjoying a simple pleasure, her family; it was rare. Sometimes she caught a glimpse at

Christmas if Paul was sober and maybe occasionally when on holiday, but from a simple jar of honey? A sense of warmth swept through her as she looked at the laughing girls. A tear came to her eye.

She picked up the jar. "There's something in the honey, Honey." She smiled and winked at her partner suggestively. "I don't think it's a honeycomb." Donna held the jar to the light before passing it across the table.

Paul took the jar and collected a fork. He put his finger in again and dotted a spot on the girls' noses. They responded with a chuckle whilst looking at Donna for approval.

"Get that with your tongues if you can, no hands mind as I find out what's in this... Yummy Hon..." He abruptly stopped speaking.

He dropped the jar, holding the object on the fork.

"Jesus Christ!" he squealed and stepped back as if something had bitten him. He let the fork and the object fall onto the table. The girls instinctively cowered.

Donna leaned away as the jar hit the table, the contents folding out of the jar's gaping mouth, almost controlled and deliberate. The amber, viscous honey crawled slowly as if trying to recapture the roughly torn square of honey-covered flesh that lay a short distance away. The girls squealed too as the honey gradually dribbled from the skin's surface, revealing the coloured markings of a section of tattoo that gradually became more visible, as the mucilaginous fluid moved from the surface to spread around it like a golden moat. Donna's involuntary gasp added to the children's sudden fear.

Chapter Five

The spit seemed to bubble as it collided with the black surface. Cyril loaded the cloth with polish and rubbed the saliva and polish in circles. If he had a pound for every time he had performed this evening ritual he would be a wealthy man. The final buff of the shoes proved worthwhile, there was a real depth to the leather's surface. He always bought shoes with a polished binder, it gave him a head start in achieving the desired shine. His colleagues had always said that criminals could tell he was a copper by the shine on his shoes. He smiled at the thought.

Shoe cleaning had always been a Sunday evening ritual as a child at home and the habit had stuck. He took a drink from the glass of *Black Sheep* before inhaling the sweet menthol vapour from his electronic cigarette. He glanced at the small painting on the wall. The dark mills looked gloomy, the tiny orange lights reflecting across the wet surface brought to mind an old case. *Hades*, he mouthed, *Just above Hades.* He shivered at the thought before moving to the window. A small cirrus cloud of vapour hung in his wake. He opened the Venetian blinds allowing light to flood the room. Robert Street was quiet. The sun illuminated the front gardens of the houses opposite; the yellow-coloured stone garden walls seemed to be absorbing the low sun's soft hue. It had been a lovely summer's day. He moved back placing the shoes on a rack before collecting the laptop bag that leaned against the wall.

Opening the laptop, he prepared to go through the files he had requested. He had been putting this off and yet he experienced a slight flutter of excitement. There had been something missed in the initial stages of the investigation he felt sure and now all he had to do was to find it.

***

The gloved hand held the jar to the light and the trapped object slid as if in slow motion across the bottom. It was added to the other identical ones on the shelf. The hand turned them precisely so that the labels all faced in the same direction. Five remained. All would have gone had the child not drawn so much attention to herself, but there would be other opportunities tomorrow and the next day. Besides, what was the rush? More jars would be added to the shelf before the end of the week. They would hold the same contents but be addressed with a different label. He closed the cupboard door.

***

The light drizzle had spoiled Cyril's daily walk to Harrogate Police Station but the umbrella had at least kept him from the worst. He peered at his shoes, the polish had done its job, there was nothing that a tissue could not solve. Cyril placed the saucer holding his china cup and a Digestive biscuit onto the mat on his desk. He set down his laptop before hanging up his jacket. Instinctively he straightened the objects on the desk whilst sipping his tea. He stared at the bagged specimen perched on the *in* tray and raised an eyebrow. David Owen knocked on the door and entered.

"Morning, sir. Good weekend?"

Cyril continued to look at the object.

Failing to get an answer, Owen tried a different tack. "Good brew, sir?"

"You're blocking the light, Owen and yes to both questions. Do sit down and explain… this." He nodded towards the object. "A present maybe from an admirer? Is it evidence or am I required to give a sample?"

Owen laughed. "It was a jar that contained honey. A rather distressed and upset chap brought it in. Contained a piece of tattooed flesh."

Cyril nearly lost the contents of his mouth but managed to swallow the tea with a choking splutter. He turned to Owen whilst returning the cup to the saucer.

"What?"

"Skin, sir, probably human. It might yet prove to be pig. It's with Forensics at present along with the honey. The jar's been checked but should remain bagged. They wanted you to look at the label, thought you'd be interested."

"What a good start to a wet Monday an empty jar in a plastic bag." Cyril recovered his composure and lifted the jar from the tray. He read the handwritten label out loud, *Bees' Kiss Yorkshire Honey*. He turned the jar and peered through the bag and the glass on the reverse of the label. "Is that a *V*, Owen?"

"Either a *V* or the Roman numeral for 5." Owen felt Cyril's eyes burn into his face. Why had he told him to what the Roman numeral corresponded? He knew better, he had worked with him long enough.

"If you look at the bottom left corner there are two faint letters, they are, and I'm accurately informed, *D* and *Q* and written in pencil." Owen pointed with his finger in the general direction.

"What was the tattoo?"

"Looks like another letter, rather ornate, but there's a small part missing suggesting that the flesh was torn rather than cut. There's a high probability that it could have been torn away using teeth. We'll know for sure once Forensics have played with it."

"And the letter?"

"Another *V* in a Gothic style. Looks more *O* to me than *V*, having a scribble-type surrounding shadow but I'm assured it's a *V*. Someone is chasing up the possible font."

"Where has the jar come from?" Cyril lifted his cup. "Are they sure it's flesh?"

Owen nodded. Cyril looked at the remains of his tea but decided to leave it.

"Are you leaving that Digestive?" Owen asked, already leaning across the desk.

Cyril offered the saucer to Owen whilst shaking his head. "Don't drop crumbs."

It was too late the whole biscuit had already vanished.

"It was given to a child at the Summer Country Show held at the Yorkshire Showground yesterday. Report is there." Owen pointed to the buff file. "Mother says the girl was given it by a man." Owen put on a staged voice. *'For a kiss like a bee'.* He picked up the report and read the statement using the same tone. '*If you kiss me like a bee kisses a flower',* the exact words the little girl told her mum, whatever that means."

"Did the mother see the man?"

Owen shook his head."

"Do you have a list of all the tradespeople at the show and all the local apiarists?"

Owen stood and came round to Cyril's computer. "May I?"

Two lists appeared. There were three people linked with bees and honey. "They're being questioned today. This is a list of all the beekeepers. There were a good number of volunteers at the show and members of the Bee Keeping Associations can sell their own produce there. However, they don't wander around swopping kisses with kids for a jar of contaminated honey. They also have to put their honey in 1lb or 12 oz jars and that, sir, is neither." Owen pointed to the jar. "It neither meets their standards of size nor labelling."

"The contents would also cause upset, I guess," Cyril murmured.

Chapter Six

12th August 2015

The choice of music was a conscious gesture that some might consider to be sensitive and caring, whilst others would argue that it was callous and controlling. Either way, the sound of *Bring Him Home* from *Les Miserables* echoed within the steel chamber as the gloved hand brushed Tony's hair away from his cold pale forehead. His eyes did not move, they stared dimly into the unknown.

"You'll like this part, Tony," a voice whispered reassuringly into his deaf ears. "Can't hear me? But then you never did and that my foolish young friend, that was your fatal error. That is how you became my boy. Music blasting in your ears made my job so much easier."

The hand smoothed the dead flesh on Tony's right inner forearm; even through the glove it felt cold and taut. He wrapped Gaffer tape carefully around the elbow and then the wrist, already severely marked by weeks of straining against the tape that had secured the arm to the wooden commode. The corpse's head lolled forward as if staring at the side table filled with strange, almost surgical pieces of equipment. Gel was squeezed onto the arm and smoothed over the flesh, bringing with it a light sheen. Next a stencil was applied containing eight letters, each running into the other owing to the intricate surrounding shading. It was left for a moment to allow the ink to mark the skin. Once lifted, it was clear to see that the spirit master ink had been transferred. It was time for the tattoo to be applied.

"Like it so far, Tony? It doesn't look much now but you wait... after all, you've all the time in the world so be patient. You'll love it and I'll be gentle, you'll not feel a thing, I promise."

The shoe hovered above the foot pedal before being slowly lowered, applying pressure to send the power to the tattoo machine. The lining needles pulsated from the tip just beyond the grip. The high-pitched buzz seemed to fill the room. He dipped the tip into red ink and the needles followed the tracing.

"I'll add a little freestyle in a minute to identify it as mine. You don't mind do you, Tony?" The tattooist's lifted gaze was turned to focus on Tony's limp face. "I thought not."

With a tissue, the gloved hand wiped away the ink as the tattoo progressed until the final letter *S* was completed.

"There Tony, it's done." He lifted his foot from the pedal and the buzzing ceased. The tattoo gun was returned to the table. "Tomorrow it will be mine and then we'll give it away bit by bit. Let's see just how clever these people really are, shall we?"

The computer's screen went dark. The tattooist moved a finger across the laptop mouse pad pressing to rewind. It was stopped to catch the final part of the film. "... How clever these people really are, shall we?" The speaker took a deep breath before the finger pressed the pad to eject the disc.

"I don't think they're very clever but we'll see, we'll see. Pity Tony's no longer here to watch his starring role." He fed a second disc into the computer, the date letters and time displayed showed twenty-four hours on from the previous disc.

It focused on the same tattooed, bound arm. This time the music had changed, *Laying down the Law* energetically sung by Paul Rogers, blasted reassuringly from some hidden speakers. He slipped a scalpel into the flesh around the edge of the tattoo, slowly sawing under the dermis as gloved fingers gradually peeled back the flesh as the blade moved back and forth. The knife's keen edge met no resistance. There was no blood. The watcher remembered the almost sweet smell blossoming from the severed skin and smiled at the memory.

"A perfect diet, Tony. A perfect diet."

Once past the tattoo the blade sliced the dermis for the last time, the tattoo was free. Skilfully, the blade then ran a small cut between each letter. The watcher leaned forward anticipating the next move. The sliver of flesh was brought into the mouth and torn with the front teeth, each careful tear separating the letters one by one. The head turned to look directly at the camera that focused solely on the mouth before taking a bow; the last piece of skin containing the final letter hung flaccidly from the grinning lips.

"You did that so well. There's a bit of the cinema in you. Not Oscar material but so enjoyable, apart that is, from your choice of music." There was a pause whilst what seemed like the same voice answered with a squealing giggle.

"Why, thank you. I should do it more often. Maybe I shall, maybe I shall... maybe my friend, I already have."

The screen went black. The disc was ejected and filed.

***

The incident room was full. Cyril glanced around at the walls paying particular attention to the gallery of photographs of Tony Thompson. In his heart of hearts he sensed that the skin sample, the honey jar and the missing youth were going to be connected. Although the room was not silent, there was very little interaction. Even that ceased when Owen entered the room. Cyril's eyes met his and the sickening feeling in the pit of his stomach intensified.

Owen leaned against the wall scanning through the iPad.

"Morning everyone. DNA says that we have a skin sample match for that of Tony Thompson. The tattoo was inked post mortem but it is a tattoo and not just an indelible marker as some thought. The skin has been flayed, again post mortem and then each letter has been torn by what appears to be teeth, although the sample held no real identifying dental marks owing to submergence in honey. It's gone to Forensic Odontology but they're not optimistic. The antibacterial qualities of the honey have preserved and therefore contaminated the sample. A true approximation of date of flaying or death is unclear at present. Again, we have to wait."

Owen looked up and flicked his finger across the touch screen.

"The honey sampled is unlikely to be English. There were traces of chloramphenicol and heavy metal contaminants which might suggest that it was sourced from China or India. Interestingly, imported honey from China was stopped in 2002 and from India in 2010."

"And the significance of chloramphenicol, Owen?" Bennett enquired.

"China had a severe infection of Foulbrood Disease that decimated the bee population. Tens of millions of bees were killed and so they used an animal antibiotic to resolve the problem. However, this drug was transferred to the honey and it is an antibiotic that can cause DNA damage in children that may trigger a rare blood disorder." Owen looked carefully before pronouncing, "Aplastic anaemia. Another banned antibiotic was found and that's Streptomycin. There was also a trace of lead, this is because the Chinese honey harvest comprises produce from thousands of peasant beekeepers who transport their honey in lead-soldered drums."

"So the honey was illegally imported?"

Owen just lifted his shoulders.

"The drug found in the vomit was also banned around 2010. What professionals are associated with banned drugs and chemicals?" There was silence. "Sarah, your task." He smiled at her. "Anyone have any thoughts on the letters pencilled on the reverse of the lab..."

Cyril's mobile rang. He answered it whilst looking at Owen. "Any marks on the back of the labels and the contents?" He noted down the information.

"Two more jars have been handed in. One was received like the first at the show, but another was in someone's shopping trolley when she loaded her car. She became a little alarmed when the skin was spread on her toast, so much so she dialled 999! She assured the officer that she didn't buy it and it wasn't marked on her receipt. She must have thought it manna from heaven." Cyril shook his head. "Strangely, the supermarket didn't sell it either. Probably dropped into the trolley by our man."

Cyril pointed to two officers one of whom was DC Stuart Park. "Stuart, get the customer's address and interview her. See what she remembers, then visit the supermarket. I want all CCTV footage for the last forty-eight hours both interior and car park if they have it. The jars are on their way to Forensics. Tattooed on the skin pieces contained in the jars we have a *C* and an *I*, so we now have *V, C* and *I* from skin samples and on the back of the labels we have *V, C, C* and the other *A, E, C.* All we need now is the entire staff of Bletchley Park or some puzzle whiz to solve this conundrum! Anyone have any bright ideas?"

Cyril looked around and noted the shaking of heads and raised eyebrows before moving towards the whiteboard. He drew three squares adding the letters and although it was not specified, he marked them in the same position as he had found them on the first label.

"Sir, would it be worth putting out a public announcement on local radio, TV and social media for people who have bought honey or received honey in the last seven days? To check if there is a foreign body, sorry! Any strange contaminant and if so to get in touch?"

Cyril nodded and smiled. Thanks, yes. Owen, see to that, please."

Owen stared at Cyril. His politeness never ceased to amaze him.

"Contact all small local shops and supermarkets to check their shelves for rogue jars. If it can be slipped into a shopping trolley or basket, it can be slipped onto a shelf. Keep everyone updated and check the computer system regularly. See too if there's any connection between those who have received a jar to date. Thanks."

Cyril moved towards Owen.

"Owen, just make the bulletin bland, no mention of labelling etc. Show me before it goes out, we want nothing that might encourage attention seekers. I also need a word regarding the files I went through over the weekend." Cyril smiled. "I read the interviews with Tony's friends who were at the fair with him. I want your thoughts." He collected his pen and pad and left.

***

Owen's desk looked like an archaeological dig it had so many layers of paper. He sat back in his chair chewing the end of a pencil when Liz Graydon stopped to chat. Liz had joined the force from Leeds and had quickly settled in. The same rank as Owen, they gelled from the word go and got along well.

"Strange case you're on. Room for one more?" Liz put on her hopeful expression.

"Supposedly we are support and nothing else although the boss seems to be squeezing his feet firmly under the table. Strange one though! Missing youth turns up in pieces in jars of honey, each torn piece carrying a tattooed letter. They seem like random letters, other letters too are written on the back of the jars' labels; we have three jars to date."

Owen passed a sheet showing the letters as they appeared on the labels.

"Have you got photographs of the letters on the skin? If torn they should make individual fits. Maybe a pattern match too. Could they be giving you a word? Is someone communicating with you?" Liz held out the sheet. "Strange the way the written letters have been located to a specific part of the labels – that's saying something to me, it's about location."

Liz dropped the sheet back onto the desk.

"Whilst you're here having fun investigating bees and honey, I'm going to deal with a persistent wife abuser who's forgotten the rules regarding birds and bees in marriage. It was ever thus!" She smiled and left.

Owen picked up the sheet, returned the pencil between his lips and watched her leave before reaching for the phone.

***

Cyril was busy making notes on a pad when Owen knocked and entered.

"You wanted to talk over the files?"

"Grab a chair. We can discount the paedophile connection at least for those in the north west. Liaison officers or whatever they're called these days, have interviewed them and none can be tied to the disappearance of the other two and none was in this area at the time of Tony's abduction. They're opening the other two as cold cases, what with better DNA sampling, you never know. Anyway, I scrutinised the interviews with the boys who were with Tony Thompson on the night that he disappeared. In both accounts they say Tony was feeling ill after the first ride but wasn't actually sick, yet strangely he was the only one who bought food. Why anyone feeling remotely queasy would contemplate eating grease and... never mind, surprises me. Interestingly he was given a bottle of fizzy drink for free and it was after eating and drinking this that he vomited."

"Sometimes sir, if I've had a bit too much to drink and then have a kebab, I throw up straight away, strange really. Happened to me a few times. Could be the reason he puked."

"You're a mine of information, Owen. What a life you lead! Remember when we flew back from Nice and you turned the colour of an avocado. If you'd seen a stall selling hot dogs would you have bought one?"

Owen remembered the occasion all too clearly. "Certainly not, I think the smell would have been enough."

"My point exactly. After alcohol you feel hungry, with motion sickness you feel the opposite. So why eat?"

"Maybe he wasn't feeling sick at all, maybe he was just messing, pretending in order to worry those friends sitting opposite or next to him," Owen commented.

"Colin Fretland said that within minutes of finishing the fizzy drink he vomited violently and said that he felt awful. Both he and Mark Webster thought it amusing to tell him he'd contracted something awful from the food that they serve at places like that. At least they had common sense. They didn't see him again. He left heading this way." Cyril turned the street map round and pointed with his finger. "That cross is where the vomit was found. As you'll know, the foot traffic around the site over the period was extremely heavy, litter was a problem too. Doesn't matter how many bins are placed it's always easier to drop it. You can imagine the work that each piece removed from the scene is taking to process. Footwear Forensics are investigating the marks as we know where Tony knelt. Forensics also traced the place where Tony initially vomited and therefore where the litterbin stood. The boys said he threw his bottle and wrapper into it and then was sick into the bin immediately afterwards. The bin was cleared away by the organisers and although it has rained since then, they have recovered traces of his DNA and Toxicology found traces of the drug Ipecac from spatter."

"The improved DNA-17 tests seem to be able to find a needle in a haystack." Owen grew quite animated. "Really impressive especially with cold cases."

"Take Liz and interview these." Cyril slid a piece of paper over the desk. "They all had food outlets at the fair. Find out who gave away drinks with the food and find out where they were located. Here's a plan of the site. You're looking for ones in this area." Cyril handed over photographs taken from the site of the litterbin. "The Crime Scene Manager assures me that the photographer's position and camera direction for those images are marked on this aerial view of the scene. It gives a clear perspective of where all of the elements of the fair were sited; the grass discolouration shows areas covered by equipment. You can see the various rides superimposed and the food outlets, but which ones stood where, for some reason, is uncertain."

"I thought we were purely support, sir and that Liz..." Owen did not finish. Cyril's raised eyebrow above his glasses was enough. Owen knew better. "Sir!"

Owen spread the photographs on an empty table to orientate himself with the scene and then called Liz. "It's Owen. Listen, *Flash* has invited you to the party. Can you meet me outside in the car park within the hour?" He did not receive an answer he just heard her laugh in delight.

***

Liz drove. She turned the unmarked car onto Otley Road moving slowly through town before turning onto the A59. Bilton Lane came up on the right. It was a long road bordered by a variety of fairly modern houses.

"What are we looking for?" Liz lowered her speed to less than thirty.

"Woodfield Road... turn here. There, the bungalow with the van."

Owen checked the address with that written on the sheet on his knee. "We're looking for a Mr Jenkins, a Bruce Jenkins. Ready?"

Owen showed his ID and a lady opened the door a little wider. "He's in bed."

Liz looked at her watch. "It is urgent and hopefully we'll not need to return."

"Come in, I'll get him. Go through there and make yourselves comfy."

They could hear the conversation across the hallway.

"I'll need a minute, make them a brew."

Bruce Jenkins came into the lounge wrapped in a tartan dressing gown. Somehow Owen had expected him to be younger. He glanced down at his notes. He was fifty-three but considering his girth, his bald head and skin tone he looked ten years older. Owen stood and proffered a hand.

"DS Owen and this is DS Graydon." He looked more bemused.

"Sorry!" He pointed to his clothing. "You see my work takes place late in the day and at my age I need to catch up."

Owen glanced down at Jenkins's bare feet. The toenails were brown through fungal infection and the nails needed cutting. He then looked at his tattooed hands before his eyes settled on his badly bitten fingernails.

"Is something wrong?" Bruce Jenkins's voice seemed to break Owen's stare.

Owen passed him the plan of the fair. "Where was your stand positioned at the Stray Fair, Mr Jenkins?"

He took the paper, leaned forward, scooped a pair of reading glasses from the coffee table and peered at the plan. He began turning his head to the side as if trying to work out which way it should be.

"There!" his stubby finger pointed to the plot furthest from where the litterbin Tony had used was positioned.

"Do you know the other food traders, Mr Jenkins?"

He nodded. "Regulars round town. The competition," he said with a smile and a rare degree of humorous animation, before looking at both Owen and Liz.

"How stiff is the opposition, Mr Jenkins?"

"It's not really, we tend to price together otherwise we'd make nothing. Some just add a few more onions but we're much the same."

"Free drink to entice the punters, hot dog and free fizzy drink?" Liz asked.

The look he returned said everything. "Does this lass know Harrogate's in Yorkshire?" A broad smile spread across his lips for the second time since their arrival. "*Give... free...* those words are not in my vocabulary, love."

"Employees?"

"I have one assistant. The wife used to help but with her bad back she can't any more."

"Who's that?"

"Pam, Pamela Shepherd. Lives at Hampsthwaite."

"What about the others traders?"

"Tend to use casual staff, students and the like, cheaper, cash in hand. They pay nowt too."

"Thanks, we'll not keep you any longer. It's a long shot but do you recall that a youth went missing during the fair? Here's a picture. Do you remember seeing him or serving him?"

Jenkins looked at them both. "I've seen his picture on the telly and in the paper. Do you know how many people we saw during the time there? Bloody thousands and you expect me to remember one. Sorry, most days can't remember what I had for my tea last night let alone a face in a crowd!"

"If you do remember anything, no matter how trivial you might believe it to be we'd appreciate a call. Keep this, it has DS Owen's contact details." Liz smiled and placed the small card into his hand.

Owen and Liz left.

"Onward and upward. Now to see a Gary Barton and then to finish the day, we have a Mrs Sonja James. Lovely!"

Chapter Seven

Cyril placed the photographs of the skin tattoos on the white boards and was trying to match the shadow pattern and the tears. Someone was whistling lightly in the background. He moved the images until he felt sure two lined up before looking at the accompanying document. Forensics had confirmed the match. So he had *VI* and a rogue *C*. All he had to do was to see if there was a word whilst not knowing the number of letters. But then again they might represent Roman numerals. He took out his electronic cigarette and stared at the board. A plume of white vapour appeared from his right nostril.

DC Park came in and saw Cyril staring at the letters. "Would you like a *P*, sir? Playing *Countdown*?"

Cyril laughed. "Even without a television I get that, Stuart. It would be a bit easier, believe me. Anything?"

"Lady saw nothing, she just found the jar in her trolley and then the contents. The car park and shop CCTV has gone for analysis. Should be with us by the end of shift."

"I've been through Tony's social media pages. His phone record stops the evening of his disappearance. It was turned off or destroyed some time before midnight when there was a number of calls from his frantic parents."

"The letters are a key... but..." Cyril's mobile rang interrupting his sentence.

"She's here?" Cyril asked. "I'm on my way down." Cyril covered the mouthpiece and looked at Stuart. "Woman's called in to say that her daughter was given a jar of honey at the Country Show. Says she noticed it contained something so she threw it away, didn't open it." He spoke again into the phone. "I'll need a WPC with me."

***

Mrs Wilson waited in the reception area. A glass of water had been placed on the coffee table.

"Mrs Wilson?" Cyril asked. He noticed that he had startled her. She seemed deep in thought.

"Sorry. Thank you for waiting. I'm DCI Bennett and this is WPC Stapleton." Cyril showed her through to a more private lounge area. "I believe you or your daughter received a jar of honey from a stranger?"

"Yes, yes, my daughter. One minute she was with me the next she'd gone. It's not like her she's normally shy. She told me that a man called her. He was holding out the jar. She said that she gave him a kiss and he gave her the jar of honey. She still says he was very kind and nice. This isn't making sense is it?"

"If it's any consolation, this also happened to other little girls on two occasions over the weekend that we know about. This may sound an irrelevance considering the circumstances but it's very important. Can you describe the label on the jar, Mrs Wilson?"

She laughed and relaxed a little. "The irony is, it was called *Bees' Kiss Honey*. The label seemed handwritten. There was something in the honey, goodness knows what, so I threw it away. I thought nothing of it until hearing the news and your request for information. Strange, made me go all fluttery."

"Two things, did your daughter describe the man?"

"Mr Bennett, she's six. She said that he was kind that he had a white beard and twinkly eyes."

"Where did you dispose of the jar?"

"I put it in the first litterbin that we came to."

Cyril looked at the WPC and then returned his gaze to Mrs Wilson. "You did the right thing." He smiled, lying to be polite. "Again thanks. We have your details but I don't think we'll need to see you again. If you'd like one of our Community Police Officers to pop in with some *Stranger Danger* picture books and chat to…?"

"Emilie."

"... Chat to Emilie, I'd be happy to organise that." Cyril smiled and stood. "Thank you again, Mrs Wilson."

Stuart Park was still in the incident room when Cyril returned.

"Same jar and label as before but unfortunately the mother disposed of it at the show ground. Check who had the contract for waste disposal for the Country Show, see if a recycling programme was used. If it's tendered to an outside contractor then check where glass or general waste was taken. Long shot but you just might find the proverbial needle."

***

Liz and Owen arrived at their final interview. Capthorne Avenue backed onto a trailer park. Liz looked into the overgrown garden and pulled a face at Owen.

"I don't think Alan Titchmarsh is home or has been for a few years! Let's get it over with."

They eased past a dilapidated car that almost blocked the driveway, sitting unloved and partially hidden under a blue tarpaulin. The net curtain twitched before they reached the door. Both Liz and Owen saw the movement and waited for the entrance to open. A large lady appeared with a distinctly sour demeanour.

"We're buying nowt at the door so ya can bugger off!"

Liz looked at Owen and a cynical smile broke across her lips as if inviting Owen to speak. He did not. He removed his ID and held it up for the woman to read.

"Jesus, what's he done now?"

"Are you Sonja James?"

The woman backed away a little and nodded.

"May we come in?"

Owen entered first, this time his lack of manners being justified. The strong smell of wet dog and fried food stung their nostrils. Owen looked at the chaos of the sitting room and remained in the hallway.

"Did you have a food outlet at The Stray Fair?"

She nodded. Since seeing Owen's ID she had apparently turned mute.

"I take it that your spot at the fair was..." Owen showed her the plan and photographs. "... here. Is that correct?"

"Yes, there. Wasn't a good location really. Barton's had best un but then he paid that bit more. He didn't open on a couple of days, had some technical problems." She chuckled. "Couldn't happen to a nicer chap. We did alright. What's up any road?"

"We? You were not serving alone, you employed someone?"

"I had two helpers, part time, friends like. They help me and I help them. It can get a bit busy. I need someone doing tea, coffee whilst I concentrate on the food, so they did split shifts like."

"Pay tax, did they? Everything legal and above board?" Liz asked in an unthreatening manner but she knew it was a Trojan Horse question.

There was a long pause as Sonja's facial colour changed. "They're friends, they helped for nowt like friends do."

"Did you give free fizzy drinks with food, Sonja?"

"Funny you should ask that, we did. A guy gave us a crate of drinks, said it was an energy drink under trial and that they'd be interviewing people they saw with the plastic bottle. We had about twenty-four, maybe a few more, not sure now. Gave us a tenner for handing it out. I tried one and it were crap."

"Did it have a name this energy drink?"

"*Ichor*, remember it as clear as day. Thought it'd not do as well as others with such a daft name. Looked cheap too. Oh aye, he said only to give it to teenagers, not adults and only to lads 'cos that were the market they were targeting." She lifted her shoulders. "For a tenner I'd 've drunk the bloody lot myself."

"Two things. I want the names and addresses of your helper friends and I want you to give me a full description of this chap who gave you the drinks to distribute and any documentation that he gave you."

"Last question's easy 'cos he gave me nowt only the drinks and a tenner. You know it's a long time since. I think I can describe him and I'd appreciate it if you could leave my friends out of this."

Owen shook his head. "Here or the station? Your call."

"OK! We'll do it here. I really didn't have the time to chat to him. He just dumped them on the floor and handed over the tenner. One thing I did notice though, he was a bit of a fairy."

"Sorry?"

"Tha knows, a bit gay like. Had a white goatee beard, glasses and a peaked cap with the name of the drink on it. He was at the van door for only a few minutes. I had folks to serve. One thing for sure he was tall, I'd say about six foot and slim."

Owen looked at Liz and they both knew what each was thinking.

"Your friends' names... now!"

Liz and Owen sat in the car. Owen smelled the sleeve of his jacket. "Great! Can you smell that?"

"Can smell nothing other than that house. I swear my shoes were sticking to the carpet. If the lad bought food from her, I'm not surprised he threw up."

"So, we have a man in disguise."

Chapter Eight

Early September

The informal five-a-side was intense even though the match was drawing to a close.

"Next goal wins!" shouted one of the players.

Carl Granger kicked the ball from the imaginary wing and found the head of Curly Brewer and from that point on the game was finished; it was a certain goal.

"Bloody hell, Pelter, ya daft, blind sod, I could've saved that with me knob end!"

"If ya think I'm divin' in this, Scotty," he grumbled, pointing at the muddy grass, "when I have my good stuff on, you've another think coming. You go in goal if you're not happy."

Carl and Curly just laughed and gave each other a celebratory hug. A tall figure crossed The Stray and watched the game briefly before dropping the plastic bottle next to the screwed-up jacket that formed one of the far goal posts. He quickly turned and walked away. The sound of laughter diminished until it blended with the noise of the far traffic. All the boys were watching the antics at the other goal and as they were playing goalie when needed, the opposite goal where the lone spectator once stood was empty.

"Two one, Pelter, Scott said next goal wins!" they shouted.

Scott grumbled angry that he had made that call. "Let's have one more and then that's it."

"Loser!" the opposition chanted before running up and patting him on the back. "Tomorrow, we'll have a rematch. It's getting late. I'm off."

The spectator stood some distance away propped against one of the many trees that ran down Stray Rein on either side of the narrow road. Here, The Stray was cut twice, once by Stray Rein, the narrow road that linked the large collection of houses to the A6040, and by the main Leeds to Harrogate railway that sat low in the tree-lined cutting. A small, grass-covered bridge allowed crossing of the cut.

"Is this anyone's?" Pelter held up the plastic bottle. "It was on my jacket."

"It's probably yours. You just don't remember putting it there. Can't see the ball heading towards the nets and he can't remember what he brought with him!" The boys laughed.

Pelter held it up. It was full. He just lifted his shoulders and laughed. "Anyone want a swig?"

Carl Granger took it and twisted off the top before putting it to his lips. He tipped back his head and drank half the bottle.

"Bloody hell, Granger! Leave some!" Pelter grabbed the bottle back.

"That's foul!" Carl Granger exclaimed wiping his mouth. "No wonder you're crap at football if you drink that." He bent down untangling the clothing that had formed the goal posts, tossing a jumper to Curly before slipping his own over his shoulders.

Pelter finished the bottle and then threw it in the air before kicking it. Curly picked it up and proceeded to try to keep it in the air. They applauded when he managed twenty kicks.

"Put it in the bin, I'm off."

The spectator watched Pelter jog off across Stray Rein heading for the grassed footbridge that crossed the railway cutting. The others dispersed in other directions. Carl picked up the plastic bottle and looked at the label. He suddenly felt a wave of nausea rise in the pit of his stomach. He let the bottle drop grabbing his abdomen.

It was then that the spectator made his decision. He moved away from the tree and crossed to retrieve the plastic bottle that lay in the grass before following the boy.

***

Cyril sat with his feet resting on a cushion that was perched on the coffee table. He was reading a book on northern artists, *A Northern School Revisited.* A glass of *Black Sheep* beer sat to his right and the mellow sound of Classic FM drifted from the radio. So far it had been a confusing week in which they seemed to have produced more questions than answers. He could not settle, he was neither taking in the music nor the written word. His mind tumbled across a minefield of different facts. Something was eluding him from one of the earlier missing person cases, he was sure of it. It would be another three hours of perusal and a second beer before his phone rang putting an end to his evening at home and his dilemma.

"Bennett."

It was Stuart Park.

"We have another missing youth. Fourteen years old, last seen over two hours ago. Should have been home at eight."

Cyril looked at his watch, shook it and looked again. It was ten fifty-five.

"Call outs and patrols are looking. His mobile's dead, last call just before eight to home to say he was just on his way. Never arrived."

"Send a car. I'm coming in."

***

Above the moans and sniffles it was clearly visible. It did not take much finding, there, in the youth's eyes, that cocktail of fear, confusion and uncertainty. Carl Granger vomited into the bucket that sat on his lap for the fifth time, very little appeared. His spontaneous retching produced only the dribbles of green bile that clung web-like, from his lips leaving fine strings of saliva. Sweat beaded his forehead.

"I take it, my young friend, that you didn't like my energy drink? But then it's not for mere mortals like your young self. Seems to work perfectly well for me."

Carl shook his head as he tried desperately to move his arms but they were bound to what looked like a wooden chair.

The steel room seemed chilled and Carl shivered, more from dehydration than fear. A bottle of water was placed to his lips and he sipped eagerly before spluttering.

"Slowly, take your time. You have lots of time now, lots and lots of it."

***

Cyril went straight to the incident room. Stuart was waiting with a full description of the boy.

"SOCO team's at The Stray now and the area has been sealed. They've found traces of vomit in surrounding areas either side of Stray Rein where the lads were playing. We await DNA and Toxicology results from the samples. We're interviewing the boys who Carl's parents said were playing football with their son. One's been taken to A&E with what appears to be severe vomiting."

Cyril never understood his total aversion to vomit. He could deal with most things and in his career he had witnessed some dreadful sights but for some reason vomit, even his own, proved a total anathema.

Stuart produced *Google Earth* on the interactive screen and pointed to the area.

"The markers for the samples found are here, here and... here. You can see that they're on either side of the road. It appears we have multiple victims. One crossed the railway cutting here. That sample was from Peter Lee, the kids know him as Pelter. He lives on West End Avenue, so he was heading in that general direction. He's presently in A&E. I have somebody there now. Initial medical thoughts are that he is suffering from severe food poisoning. Our missing lad is Carl Granger, aged fourteen. You can see he was heading in the opposite direction. All the addresses are on file. The Grangers refused an offer for an officer to remain with them overnight."

"Any witnesses other than the lads? Anyone see anything?"

Stuart shook his head. "I have a couple of officers doing general door to door and we've recorded the registration numbers of the cars parked down Stray Rein. They're being checked."

"Get alerts out and get the phones manned A.S.A.P. I'll go and see the missing boy's parents. I'll take a WPC driver... I've had a couple of beers. Get Owen and Liz in as soon as. Good work, thanks. When are you off?"

Stuart looked at his watch. "Two hours ago. I'll wait until Owen comes in."

Cyril smiled and put a hand on Stuart's shoulder before picking up the file and scanning for the address. "What you'd give for a nine till five!"

"We'd both hate it," Stuart replied, "and you know it."

"Call if there's anything."

"Nearly forgot, we've tracked down the glass recycling container from the Showground. It's in the hands of a private contractor and fortunately still at the depot. They've put it to one side. I've requested Forensics to go through it but that can't happen for another twelve hours. There's a lot of glass, sir, so what state a honey jar will be in is anyone's guess. General waste has gone to recycle or landfill disposal."

Cyril only smiled. "Get someone to keep on top of that. Thanks."

***

The lights were on when Cyril arrived at Carl Granger's home. A young woman was standing at the window staring out, her arms wrapped around her body as if seeking reassurance.

Cyril did not need to knock, the door was opened as he approached. He could see the slight optimism in the eyes of the man he assumed to be Mr Granger.

"DCI Bennett. Mr Granger?"

No, I'm his brother. Don is in the back. Anything?"

"Nothing as yet but ..." Cyril stepped inside followed by the WPC.

Don looked up as Cyril entered. "You've not found the first missing lad yet and how long's that been? So what's the chance of finding our boy?"

The maelstrom of human emotion erupted, part anger part frustration, but the general feeling was that of a desperate helplessness.

"I have just a few questions, Mr Granger. Please be assured we're working hard to locate Carl and ensure he's returned home safely. One of the boys who was with Carl is attending A&E suffering from a severe stomach upset. Was Carl fine when he left home?"

"He had his tea and went out. I like to see him enjoy the school holidays, there's only a week left. I prefer it if he's out with his mates rather than tied to his computer."

"Did you all eat the same thing?"

"Sorry?"

"Important that you answer this accurately. Did you all eat the same meal and is anyone feeling ill or any sickness?"

"We all had the same thing. We had a chicken salad and we had a few chips. We're worried sick but everyone's fine, nobody's thrown up if that's what you're asking. He was fine when he left, fine when he rang to say he was just leaving The Stray. He even joked that I should put the kettle on and get the biscuits ready!"

Cyril noticed a slight smile as Don played back the last conversation he had held with his son and then he witnessed the tear grow before it rolled down Don's cheek. He noticed the biscuits on the coffee table and the mug containing cold tea.

"This is going to be difficult but I'd like to have someone go through your son's computer, tonight if possible. We can either get one of the Forensic digital team to collect it or the task can be performed here, but it would be better back at the centre."

"It's a laptop and he's got an iPad. Take them, if it'll bring him back take them"

Don stood, wiped his face with the back of his hand and went upstairs returning with the two machines. I don't know his passwords but he's mad on aircraft so that might give you a lead."

Cyril noticed that Don had recovered some of his composure. "Sorry, bit screwed up. If there's anything else..." He lifted his hands.

Cyril made a call to organise the collection of the IT equipment. "Was your son an Air Cadet, Mr Granger?"

Don nodded. "Crackers about planes. Even his favourite cup, look!"

Cyril noticed the image of a Vulcan on the mug that was on the coffee table. He then noticed the white halo that had settled on top of the liquid and it made him think of Owen.

"It's noted that you have given the police an up-to-date photograph. Would you like a WPC to be here for your wife, Mr Granger?"

"We're a strong family, we're fine."

Cyril handed him his number. "Ring if there's anything."

Chapter Nine

Owen stood on Stray Rein and looked at the three enclosed areas. Temporary lights had been set up and the thrum of two generators whispered above the occasional traffic noise. The technicians, dressed in their protective suits, moved cautiously if not a little eerily around the scene. The occasional flash of a camera illuminated the area with intense white light.

A white-suited, Crime Scene Manager walked towards Owen. "We have a plastic bottle top found where the lads played. Looking at the condition of the grass it was where they'd stored their stuff as goal posts. It's with a courier and on its way to the lab. Nothing else. Shows how clean Harrogate is!" she smiled. "Another hour to take shoe prints and we should be ready for the final walk through."

Owen looked at his watch, walked to the road and leaned against a tree. A number of people were trying to see what was going on. Owen glanced at the staring onlookers but took little notice. Whenever there was a cordon there were spectators. The local TV cameras had set up a short distance away and someone was talking to camera.

***

Cyril sipped his tea and went through the files on his desk. He read a report from Sarah detailing the process of destroying banned and unwanted chemicals and drugs. Incineration seemed the likely method. He scanned for addresses and made notes.

He checked with the Digital Forensic Unit to see if there was anything on the computers he had brought in earlier; an optimistic call but he was in need of information. Forensics had taken an image of each device to protect the content from contamination and they were searching Carl's Internet history, files and messages. They were also looking for keyword hits in deleted files. The majority of the conversation flew some distance above Cyril's head. He asked Owen to liaise with the technical boys, after all the youths seemed to understand the devil's ways more.

He read through the notes made after Owen interviewed the fast food operators. Sonja James seemed to be the most profitable for information. He stopped before highlighting the word *Ichor.*

"Ichor." He said the word over a couple of times. He had heard the word before but could not recall where. He tapped it into a search engine.

Ichor originates in Greek mythology, where it is the ethereal fluid that is the Greek gods' blood, sometimes said to retain the qualities of the immortals' food and drink, ambrosia or nectar. It was considered to be golden in colour, as well as lethally toxic to mortals. Great demigods and heroes occasionally attacked gods and released Ichor, but gods rarely did so to each other in Homeric myth.

It was like a penny falling from a great height. Cyril shook his head. *Lethally toxic to mortals*, he said to himself. He turned to Owen's report and read on. Tall, white goatee beard, similar description to that given by… he leaned across to some notes that he had made earlier. "Similar to that given by Emilie Wilson," he whispered.

Cyril's phone rang.

"Bennett." He listened. "One minute."

The jar within the recycling container had been located and the initial details were about to be given. He picked up a pen. "The label?" he added notes. "And the tattoo?" He wrote a large letter *S*. "Thanks, please let me know if you get anything else from the jar."

Now he had the letters *V, C, I* and *S* tattooed on four pieces of flesh.

"The bastard! I wonder?"

Cyril wrote underneath.

I AM THE MASTER OF MY FATE;
I AM THE CAPTAIN OF MY SOUL

If he were correct there were another four jars to find, and if his guess were right, he knew the letters tattooed and imprisoned within each.

***

Owen and Liz were reading through the notes when Cyril entered the busy incident room; Owen, as usual, looked as though he had just fallen out of bed which on this occasion was true. He noticed an enthusiasm in Cyril's expression and it made him feel even more soporific.

"Sorry for this early start and thanks for coming in, it's either late or early but not too sure myself!" Cyril smiled, picked up a marker pen and added the four letters to the whiteboard. The constant chatter of voices hummed in the background. "What word do you see? There are letters missing but does anything hit you?"

"Victorious," Liz said immediately but felt the exact opposite.

Owen tapped the details into his iPad demanding the answer from *Google*. "Hundreds," he said without a smile.

He turned the pad round and there was a list starting with those words containing eleven letters all the way to those containing six.

Cyril put his hand to his chin feeling a little deflated. "This is just an idea." He wrote the word *INVICTUS* under the letters. "It came to me immediately and I just thought our man was playing with us. It's Latin for unconquered. It's the title of a poem. I feel he's playing, he's teasing and he's testing us. The other letters on the labels' reverse have to mean something too, a code or a guide. Anyone thought anything further?"

Liz looked at Owen, she appeared unconvinced. “We really can’t make that presumption, can we?”

One of the officers called out to say that the DNA and Toxicology results were in from Stray Rein. Both samples showed concentrated amounts of Syrup of Ipecac, two samples were from the missing youth, the other from Peter Lee.

“The recovered plastic top also contained traces. They’ve checked for fingerprints but nothing other than those of Lee and Grainger. The other lads present mentioned that Peter Lee offered everyone a drink but only he and Carl Granger drank, none of the others touched it. They thought the bottle was left near where they played. After it was emptied someone kicked it. Strangely they said that Peter Lee was surprised to discover the bottle on his jacket, said he hadn’t brought it.”

“There was only the top found, no trace of the bottle. Looks like whoever placed it, removed it.”

“Have all the bins in the vicinity been checked?” Cyril asked.

“All and they did a sweep of the railway cutting too, but nothing. Council will check all other bins around The Stray. I’ve issued a description and the name *Ichor*. We’ll know tomorrow.”

Cyril explained the meaning behind the name. “It’s all linked.” Cyril looked at the board. “Anyone interviewed Pamela Shepherd?”

Liz tapped her pencil on her teeth. “It’s on my list for today along with Sonja James’s friends. We can remove Gary Barton, he didn’t open on the day Tony Thompson disappeared. His fridge and I quote, *was buggered*, caught fire the first day of the fair and so he didn’t get up and running until the day after Carl went missing.”

“I take it he’s neither six foot nor sports a white goatee?” Cyril asked tongue in cheek.

Liz smiled. “Fairy tale ending, sir, but alas…”

“We’re checking with the owners of the parked cars that were on Stray Rein today and with the radio and TV coverage we should glean something.”

Chapter Ten

Cyril looked at his watch, it was nine in the morning. He had returned home, showered and changed. It had been a long night. His mind tumbled over the progress made but they were still no closer to finding the latest victim. Cyril was both angry and amazed that in broad daylight someone could just disappear; nobody had come forward having witnessed anything out of the ordinary. Two people had rung to say they had seen the boys but there was nothing unusual in that.

He picked up his phone and dialled.

"Goodness me, it's a will-o'-the wisp!" Julie's voice was light and bubbly.

"Funny from someone who hasn't been up all night."

"So from that I take it you have? Bragging or complaining, Cyril?"

"I was going to invite you out for dinner but I find I'm now watching something on television tomorrow evening."

"You've no TV remember? Love to, what time?"

"I'll be at yours for seven." Cyril smiled to himself and hung up.

Cyril had known Julie Pritchett for a number of years and they enjoyed a casual and sometimes passionate relationship. There was no real commitment on either side as they both had a keen focus on their careers. It was more the trust and companionship they craved, but as Julie often let Cyril know, the sex had an attraction too. Dr Julie Pritchett was one of the four Home Office Pathologists working within the north east.

Cyril had barely sat down at his desk when Stuart put his head round the door.

"We've had two sightings. A man was seen helping a youth away from the place where the lads were playing soccer. Thought by the way they interacted it was a parent. He says that the man collected the lad's sweater and an object before leading him down Slingsby Walk. Seemed caring, there was no struggling or fuss. Everything appeared above board and he thought no more about it until he heard the news this morning. Description meets that of our man. I've called for door to door along St Wilfred's Road. Those houses back onto The Stray at that point. Also one of the drivers of the parked cars noticed a tall, thin chap leaning against a tree watching the lads play football. Had a jacket with a hood that was pulled up even though it was warm. He just thought it strange."

"Did the police dog not pick up that trail last night?"

"Strangely, there was nothing."

"Get a dog down there again and track away from the scene. See if it can find more vomit or a trail. I know it's a long shot but we need to grasp at straws."

***

Liz drove down Hollins Lane into Hampsthwaite stopping outside the Methodist Chapel; she checked her notes. The house she was looking for was one opposite the stone terrace just next to the chapel. She looked across at it. The upstairs curtains were drawn, the upper part of the left one hung limply as if missing rings. There was no car on the weed-filled gravel drive and the garage door yawned partly open. Liz immediately thought of the *Marie Celeste* and smiled. Would there be a steaming bowl of porridge on the table and a kettle whistling on the stove? She checked the road and crossed.

As she crunched down the drive she noticed the blinds separate in the window of the house next door. It was only a brief twitch but it was definitely a movement. Within seconds an elderly man appeared.

"Can I help you, young lady?"

Liz was rather taken aback but smiled. "Unless Pamela Shepherd lives with you and I have the wrong address..."

"Pamela's away. Wonderful thing this Neighbourhood Watch. I'm looking after her dog. He's in there." The man pointed at Pamela's door. I walk him and feed him but I'd suggest you don't knock as he'll go daft."

"Do you know where she is and when she'll be back, Mr…?"

The man shook his head. "Who are you?"

Liz had now had enough. She removed her ID and walked towards the hedge that separated the two drives and held the document with a stretched arm. "I'm DS Graydon and you are?"

The man did not even check it. "Mr Melville, John Melville. Why didn't you say you were the police and save all this dancing around? Ex force myself. Bradford, on the dogs for a while, must be thirty years now, a lifetime ago."

"So, where's Pamela Shepherd, Mr Melville?"

"Away looking after her aunt. She hasn't set a return date but rings me every couple of days to check on the dog."

"Where's the aunt live?"

"Ilkley. Poor girl finds it difficult holding down a permanent job because of the toing and froing. I believe she gave up teaching and then came here to look after her mum. When she passed away, she told me that she'd promised her mum that she'd look after her sister. Think it's some kind of dementia but she doesn't like to talk about it too much. Know what though? There'll be no one to look after her when it's all done. Not been back for some time. As kind and caring as they come that lass."

"Do you have a number on which we can contact her? We just need to clear some information about the missing youths that you've probably read about."

He disappeared into the house and Liz noticed a bicycle leaning in the hallway. She looked back across at her car and the stone terrace row running down the main village road. She squinted to read the name that was partially hidden by a downspout, *Clarence Terrace*.

John Melville returned with the number.

"You know the garage door's open?" Liz commented as she added the number to her phone.

"It's jammed, neither opens nor shuts. Nothing in to steal anyway. The dog warns me if anyone goes down the side of the house. Go on, try."

Liz walked towards the garage to be met by the crashing of what sounded like a large dog hitting the front door, its bark deep giving the impression it was a dog of size.

"Rottweiler called Sam, soft as anything, his bark's worse than his bite. I take him out a couple of times a day, let's say it helps bring back happy memories."

The dog continued to bark until John called its name. "See, soft."

Liz thanked him and returned to the car. She would call the number when back at the station. Within a minute of driving away her mobile rang. Pulling to the roadside she noticed it was Owen.

"Hi, all OK?"

"Two more jars have turned up and it looks as though *Flash* might be right. We have *N* and *I* added to the list but it depends on how many pieces we're looking for. I've checked and we could have INCIVISM, CIVILIANS and dare I say, VIVISECTING? Strangely, Liz, there are no letters in the corner of the labels' reverse but a *zero* and an *I* in the centre."

"On my way."

***

When Liz arrived in the incident room, a new whiteboard contained the letters and a photograph of the reverse of the labels made to form a grid pattern. Four words were written on the board: INCIVISM – neglect of duty as a civilian, CIVILIANS – self-explanatory, VIVISECTING – the act of vivisection and INVICTUS – unconquered.

"There's possibly hundreds if there are many more jars to find," Owen whispered, making her jump.

"Yep, as long as the longest piece of human flesh belonging to a fourteen-year-old," Liz answered. She did not turn but continued to stare at the letters and the words. "I think

Flash is right, it's usually the first thing that comes to you and right now that statement is certainly true." Her finger tapped the board beneath INVICTUS. "Why is he unconquered, what battles has he faced, if at all it is a he? But what of the others? We now have a *zero*, and is that *O* or *zero* on the first label?"

Owen moved away from his desk and stood next to her.

"Can we turn them all into numbers? Take the alphabet, *A* being one." He scribbled down the alphabet and added their sequential number. "We would have *V* equalling 22, *D* equalling 4 and *O* is 15."

"What if *V* represents 5, *D* 4 and it's zero not an *O*, we end up with all numbers under ten. Therefore, we have 5,4,0. But why go to all this trouble? What's the bloody point unless he's directing us or giving clues?"

"I'll tell you what you have." Owen rubbed his chin and then moved his fingers to the letters in turn. "There, clear as day."

"What is?"

"Can't you see? He's giving you the name of a well-known stately home..."

"Which is?"

"Bugger all." Owen just grinned as Liz slapped his arm. "Coffee?"

Liz smiled, nodded and then shook her head as if pretending to scream. "Thanks. I need to make a call that will hopefully make more sense than this lot."

The phone rang four times before the answerphone kicked in. It was a standard message. Liz made notes concerning Pamela Shepherd on a post-it note, adding her full name, Pamela Samantha Shepherd and tagged it to her computer screen. She would chase that later after calling Pamela again.

***

"We've found two more vomit traces, the last was in the kerb at Roslyn Road. That's a good distance from where the witness saw the man help the boy. It's also restricted parking and so if the child were abducted by car there might be a sighting. I've organised a mail drop and then a door to door for later today when most people will be home." Stuart sounded breathless. "Forensics have taken samples and results will be with you as soon as."

***

The container seemed cold even though the morning sun had hit the roof. The light entering made Carl lift his head and look but then avert his eyes from the bright light and the silhouetted figure blocking the door.

"Good morning, Carl. It's a beautiful day. Look, the sun is shining and all is well. I've brought you this."

The tape was removed from Carl's left wrist and a jar of honey was put into his hand before the strapping on the right wrist was cut.

"You have five minutes. I shall empty your mess when I return. Eat up, you know you need it!"

Carl stared at the face looking down at him, the eyes seemed warm and friendly but how could that be?

Chapter Eleven

Richard Taylor walked to the end of Woodfield Road turning onto Bilton Lane. The sun was warm and the two Lakeland Terriers pulled on their connecting leads, eager to reach the track of the disused railway. At seven in the morning there was already a large estate car unpacking two black Labradors.

Richard unclipped Bella and then Sky, mother and daughter and they darted along the straight track, noses scenting the ground, docked tails moving like bees' wings. The walk would take about forty-five minutes with their destination being Nidd Park, then it would be coffee and return. This was the regular Sunday walk come rain or shine.

The gate to Nidd Hall was always inviting. The tarmac driveway ran snake-like up to the imposing hall. Once the parkland had stretched for two hundred and fifty acres, a private estate belonging to a Bradford wool merchant that he had built on the site of an Elizabethan Manor house. The grand park was significantly smaller, comprising just twenty-five acres and the hall was no longer a private residence but a hotel and leisure centre. Progress!

Richard approached the balustrade bridge where the sweeping driveway crossed the narrow Town Street. He stopped and watched his two dogs disappear down the banking and along to a stone wall. He called them but they disappeared into the thick nettles and undergrowth. Leaning on the parapet, one foot on a baluster, he watched the moving greenery as the dogs worked unseen. Trees lined both sides of Town Street at this point before culminating in a large copse to the left of the lane. The increased growling and yelping meant that the dogs had probably tracked a rabbit or hedgehog. Opening his rucksack, he took out a thermos flask and poured a coffee before again searching for movement in the undergrowth for his dogs. He could hear them but not see them. He loved this brief moment, the warm coffee revitalising his weary limbs.

Two Lycra-clad cyclists peddled below the bridge. One stopped.

"Do you have two brown dogs?" one yelled up, her wrap-around sunglasses reflecting bright yellow and concealing her eyes.

Richard nodded.

"They're pulling something apart in the siding, just down there. You should keep them on a bloody lead."

Richard could see the anger in her face but shook his head, wondering why people just do not mind their own business. He threw the remnants of his coffee away, placed the rucksack over one shoulder and carefully moved down the banking towards the sound of the dogs. The nettles stung his hands and the light dappled the deep green of the thick undergrowth. He knew what he would find, they were terriers for God's sake. He had separated the dogs from many a bloody quarry but nothing had prepared him for the sight that stared back at him.

***

Cyril turned off Ripley Road. Cones and a parked police vehicle blocked Town Street. If there was ever an incorrect name for a road, then this was it. The narrow lane ran from the main road to the rear of Nidd Hall. Flanked on one side by natural parkland, the other farmland, sentinel-like trees ran on either side, giving way occasionally to the odd stone-built house and cottage. Cyril stopped, lowered the window and smiled at the officer. "How far up?"

The officer leaned in. "A few hundred yards on the right, sir."

Cyril saw the blue and white cordon and parked a short distance from the turning where the tape belted the trees. He slipped on a pair of blue, protective overshoes and then inhaled deeply on his electronic cigarette, the menthol taste filling his mouth. It was such a beautiful morning and such a delightful spot. Cyril shook his head and looked at Liz. "Why here of all places?" Cyril asked but he knew that there would be no logic to this. Liz said nothing.

The tape had been placed around the parking area and Town Street was now closed to the public. Two police officers watched the periphery of the cordoned area. Cyril showed his ID, the officer logged his and Liz's details and then noted the time before Cyril slipped under the tape. Liz waited outside the tape; they needed as few people as possible trampling the area until the SOCO team had done its work.

She sidled up to the officer. "Where's Richard Taylor?" she asked.

The young officer pointed up the road. "He's by the bridge just round the corner. Medics are with him. He's had quite a shock. They're looking after the living, nothing for that poor bugger." He flexed his head as if pointing to the body in the undergrowth. "I have Taylor's initial statement here." He passed Liz his notebook.

Cyril leaned over the twisted remains of the body. He knew immediately that it was Tony Thompson, even by just looking through the thick, torn transparent plastic at the naked remains. The body seemed smaller than he had envisaged. He lifted his gaze and noticed somebody standing some distance away taking photographs. "Bloody Press!!" he said out loud before shouting, "Liz!"

Liz turned to see Cyril pointing at the lone figure. She responded immediately by jumping the wall and fence and moved towards the cameraman.

Cyril looked back at the cocoon-like figure. To the right of the corpse was a jar, the same as the others. He did not touch it but bent down to see if he could read the label. Owing to its position he could only read '...Kiss Honey'. He stood and walked to the office careful to retrace his initial pathway.

"Anything when you arrived?"

"Mr Taylor was with his dogs, he was shaking and obviously upset. When I checked the body I noted the tracks and prints, so kept away to the left. One thing seems strange though, sir, there was this sweet smell, appeared to come from inside the bag. Mr Taylor also noticed it on the dogs, like honey but then there's a jar dumped by the body. Possibly it could have come from that. I've noted it in my initial findings."

"I want that kept quiet, understand?" Cyril lifted his eyes to look at the reporter who was now in deep conversation with Liz.

The officer looked affronted as if the DCI thought him a rookie.

Cyril, realising his comment had caused offence, lifted his hand. "Sorry, no matter how many times you see a body, particularly a child's..." Cyril did not finish but smiled, embarrassed. "Anyone else been here that you know of?"

"Mr Taylor mentioned that two cyclists saw the dogs attacking something in the copse but he believes they thought it was an animal. He didn't think that they stopped. Apparently gave him the rounds of the kitchen for not having the dogs on a lead."

The two vans marked *Crime Scene Investigation* arrived followed by a saloon car, a blue light on the dashboard flashed its intention. Cyril recognised the car and the driver but not the passenger.

"Cyril, you seem to attract the dead. Should I be flattered or mortified?" Dr Julie Pritchett smiled, remembering their Friday night liaison. She moved to the rear of her car and changed, collecting a small black case.

"Do you know Hannah Peters, our new technician?"

Cyril held up his hand.

"Do we have a name?"

Cyril nodded. "Looks like the first missing youth, Tony Thompson. Julie there's a jar next to the body. When you've done what you have to do, can I see it?"

Julie smiled. "When I've done what I have to do you may."

Cyril noted the grammatical correction and smiled.

"Enjoyed Friday. Thanks again." She thought she saw Cyril blush slightly.

The Forensic Team started to move towards the body, placing numbered markers and photographing the full area. Julie followed them in with Hannah acting as her assigned photographer. Cyril removed his gloves and overshoes before walking towards the bridge looking for Richard Taylor.

As he approached, he could see the man looked unwell. Not a pleasant start to a Sunday for anyone. The medics were clearing away and Richard was perched on the low wall whilst the two dogs, curled at his feet, jumped up as Cyril approached. He showed his ID.

"You've had a nasty shock, Mr Taylor. I've organised a car to get you home. I take it you saw no one other that the cyclists?"

"That's right, always quiet here on Sunday at this hour. Walk here every week." He shook his head. "Bloody shock, I can tell you. Looked like a large bagged doll. Took me a while to realise what it was. Is it one of the missing boys?"

"We'll have to wait till the scientists do their thing."

Cyril continued to question him but soon realised that there was little he could bring to the investigation. Within fifteen minutes his DNA and fingerprints were sampled and he was in a police car and heading home. At the same time, two liaison officers were heading to break the news to Tony Thompson's parents.

Cyril walked back and watched the methodical progress of the Forensic Scene Investigators. Vapour clouded the air by his mouth as he drew on his electronic cigarette, giving the appearance that it was a cold day. Liz approached.

"I've been to every house down the road and requested any CCTV recordings they have. Those cameras facing Town Street might have caught passing vehicles. We'll move towards Nidd Hall once this has been cleared away. I've sent for a list of all those who registered at the hotel over the last five days and those club members who use the facilities. The Leisure Centre check-in and out system is computerised so should be immediate."

Cyril nodded as he watched the white-suited figures.

Julie lifted the tape and walked over to Cyril. She held a plastic bag in one hand.

"The jar you wanted to see. *Bees' Kiss Honey.* Label's a little smudged but it all appears intact. Interesting contents."

Cyril took the bag and held it up for inspection. "It's the same as the others." He looked more closely at the object trapped within the honey before passing it to Liz.

"Well doctor, tell me it's not what I think it is," Cyril asked whilst pulling a face that showed his disgust.

"A tattooed tongue. Definitely removed after death but tattooed before removal. The tattoo reads, *Out of... comes lies!* and from that, Cyril, one can assume the interpretation is, *Out of the mouths of babes... come lies!* I'm not a policewoman but even I think you have some nutcase seeking revenge. Whoever did this spent a good deal of time in the planning, and from where I'm looking it's not a spur of the moment abduction. Something else, there's a strong sweet smell trapped within the plastic and going by the jar and the general condition of the body, I'd predict that your boy's eaten nothing but honey since he was taken. Have either of you heard of a Mellified Man?"

Cyril looked at Liz who simply shook her head.

Julie collected the bag. "I suggest you look it up. Colin Pearson is your Area Forensic Manager, he'll have more information for you. I'll know more once we've done an autopsy but it isn't going to be easy. Can't give you a time of death yet either. There's also a slight trace of Hypochlorous Acid." Julie could interpret Cyril's look of curiosity. "Stabilised hypochlorous acid solutions are now routinely used in the NHS to prevent microbial infection within hot and cold water systems. They're great at destroying anything organic and therefore DNA but they need careful handling. It's also found in water treatment and swimming pool maintenance. It's basically a disinfectant. We're being rather cautious with the corpse at this stage, as we don't yet know what we're dealing with. Remember, chlorine is a disinfectant and look what that did as a gas in 1915! Maybe that info is a start? As I say, given time, I'll have more." She smiled and went back beyond the tape.

"Julie!" she stopped and turned. "Anything, just give me anything that might provide a clue as to where he might have been held. I can do nothing for Tony, only concentrate on Carl Granger."

"Possibly water treatment. Once I've identified the chemical I can be more positive. As soon as, Cyril, as soon as."

Chapter Twelve

Cyril typed into Google the term *Mellified Man* and began to read. He then printed the item and dropped a copy on Owen's desk. He needed a stiff drink but a coffee would have to do. Julie's words kept running around his head mingling with his recent understanding of the term mellified. Picking up the sheet he read it again.

The subject does not eat food he only partakes of honey. After a month he only excretes honey (the urine and faeces are entirely honey) and death follows.

His mind flipped to the mental image of the youth wrapped almost mummy-like in the plastic bag. He remembered the smell and the jaundiced complexion. He picked up the phone. "As soon as, yes, all the water processing plants in this area, there surely can't be too many, also swimming pools both private and public. Thanks."

Cyril tapped the desk as if either searching for patience or understanding before he stood, collected his jacket and left.

***

For Cyril, Julie's office was filled with the kind of ornaments that should only be visible to students of medicine. He really did not care to think too much about them. He let his fingers touch a glass jar containing what looked like a small sausage. Julie entered with two mugs of coffee.

"Sorry Cyril, no cups or saucers. That's a pickled penis if you're interested." She raised an eyebrow and gave him a wicked look. "Ex-boyfriend…" She noted Cyril's look and quickly added, "joke, a funny!"

Cyril did not seem amused.

"Sorry! The boy. I've never seen anything like it and neither from the records has anyone else. From the evidence it's a rough attempt at mellification. Originally it was a sacrificial offering to help one's fellow men and there are some, as I'm sure you've read, who believe the whole thing to be a load of baloney. Anyway, rather than dumping the wrapped body in some turning area, it should have been submerged in a bath of honey for a century and then broken into minute pieces and sold as a cure all for an exorbitant fee."

Cyril immediately thought of Harrogate's Royal Hall, originally known as the *Kursaal* during its Spa town heyday. It derived the name from the German meaning Cure Hall.

"Are you OK, Cyril?" Julie leaned forward and put her hand on his knee.

"Yes, sorry just went off on a mental tangent for a second. So, excuse my ignorance but what's the cause of death?" Cyril sipped his coffee. It had been a good number of years since he had been as confused as he now was.

"He was poisoned. If you take too much of anything, Cyril, it will kill you." She looked at the electronic cigarette in his top pocket. "Including that."

Cyril looked down at his pocket and then lifted his eyebrows.

"Honey is a desiccant; it sucks the moisture out of tissue and kills microbes. It encourages a slow death, close to dehydration but at the same time alters the body's metabolism, best described as mummifying and therefore it's impossible to give an accurate time of death. One thing, although it's a slow death as I've mentioned, the lad will have gradually slipped into a coma as various organs closed down and he would have known little of his fate. The area on the forearm where the tattoo was made is clearly visible."

Julie stood and turned on the wall screen bringing up photographs of the evidence from the many thumbnail images that regimentally surrounded the screen.

"This one." She enlarged it. "Shows some previous scarring and healing. You'll understand the significance of this in a minute. Note too the bruise marks to the wrist and just below the elbow. The boy was secured for most of the time he was held captive, probably until he was incapacitated. The partial glossectomy, the removal of the tip of the tongue, was post death. There was very little bleeding."

"And the scars?" Cyril had stood and moved closer to the screen.

Julie removed a pen drive from a bag and inserted it into the side of the screen. She pressed play. Cyril could see a shadowy figure partially concealing a frightened-looking youth. There were no sounds and the room was dull. The camera seemed focused on the youth's right arm that was strapped to what looked like the chair's wooden arm. The fine scalpel blade shone as it moved towards the taut flesh. Cyril watched it slice, opening the skin allowing beads to pulse to the surface before rolling round the arm. The hooded head seemed to bow reverently towards the crying youth. When the head lifted he understood fully what had taken place. He was then startled by the sudden sound of a voice.

"You're not sweet enough yet my young friend. Maybe it will take another week, maybe a fortnight but we're in no rush are we? And the only thing you get from rushing is chance-children. That's my father's advice you know and yes, I did have parents although I'm sure you might think only a bastard could keep you locked away from the world."

The screen went blank.

"It was in his oesophagus. The severed, tattooed tongue and the placement of this small pen drive in the throat are significant. Before you ask, video and voice analysis is being done at the Jeffreys' Building as we speak. What I do know is that the recording has been tampered with electronically so you're not hearing his true voice."

"Anything from saliva DNA? Other injuries?"

Julie shook her head. "Sounds ironical but the body was well cared for, clean and hair brushed. No evidence of sexual interference either. The sealing in the bag was methodical. Had it not been for the dogs it would have been intact. Now this is important. Remember I said that the body had been cleaned, well the initial assumption was correct. Hypochlorous Acid has been used to destroy any contaminating DNA and although it's a stabilised form it's unusual. If you recall I said that it was antiviral and antifungal." Cyril nodded his head feeling as though he were back at school in a Chemistry lesson. "Well I can assure you it is, it's amazingly 99.9999% effective against pathogens but it seems totally safe to handle. It's the stability and safety that make it unique. All we have to do is find out the name of the manufacturer and then there's the possibility of making a trace. I also believe he was double bagged. Once the body was placed at Nidd Hall, the outer sheath was taken off; it would have collected traces from the transport vehicle and therefore removed. Thorough!"

Cyril's phone rang.

"Shit… I'm on my way. Is Owen there? Get Liz too."

Julie placed the pen drive into a bag and slid it across the table. "Report is already with you." She tapped the computer. "Problem?"

"Another jar of honey has been found, but with a new label. It's a different size and surprisingly has new contents. Watch this space." He stared at Julie for a moment before collecting the bag containing the pen drive and left.

***

It was a déjà vu moment for Cyril as he walked into his office and saw the jar, secure in the plastic bag and nestled on his in tray.

"Everything's in bags, even the bloody body!" he groaned out loud.

"Owen!" Cyril called, picking up the bagged jar and rotating it whilst holding it to get a clear view. Owen's bulk blocked the light of the doorway. "Where, when and how?"

"It was handed in at Craven Lodge." Craven Lodge was the police station in Harrogate's town centre. "Details are there. It was found sitting on a wall a few yards from the office and brought in by a Fred Ainsworth, who thought it might be significant after reading about our request for jars of honey. His details are there also."

Liz knocked and came in. "You were nearly right, Owen."

Owen frowned.

"You said the letters on the back of the jars would lead to bugger all, well you were close, so very close. They were, in fact, the co-ordinates for where the body was dumped... Nidd Hall. Close but no..."

"You're kidding me?"

Liz put the paper on the desk and arranged the labels in a certain order before writing down the co-ordinates. She then demonstrated how the different labels made up those ordered numbers.

"That's why some of the labels had no specific numbers to the bottom left. The significance of their always being in the same location on the label gave someone a clue and only when Forensics sent in images of the body with the exact co-ordinates did we put two and two together."

"Sadly, days too late." Cyril's tone deflated the excitement that had been in Liz's voice. "So, what do we have on this jar?"

"A new label as you can see, 'Imbroglio Honey, 2015".

"What on earth is imbroglio?" Liz asked trying to gain her composure.

Owen lifted his shoulders.

"It means confusion, or embarrassing situation and that, my dear friends, is where we find ourselves. This jar was placed near the police office to be discovered and found quickly. Someone is laughing at us right at this moment."

***

Colin Pearson, the Area Forensic Manager, watched the final part of the video showing Tony Thompson's captor before pressing the pause button. He turned to address those in the room.

"We've been able to identify that whatever room Thompson was held in had metal sides and roof so was probably some kind of shipping container. Colour, probably blue, on the inside at least." Colin pointed to the top left of the screen. "If you look carefully here, you'll just make out a series of tally marks, possibly white chalk, possibly the number of days he was held captive? You will also notice the perpetrator was right-handed when using the knife. However, our handwriting expert is convinced that someone who is left-handed wrote the labels. It poses a couple of questions, either two people or our man is ambidextrous, something we cannot determine at this time. Voice investigation suggests that the sound was dubbed onto the tape at a later date and voice changing software was used. These are readily available to download free. One you might like to check out pays reference to a bee! We're checking those."

"Are you sure it's a man?" Stuart asked whilst chewing his pencil.

"Most of the descriptions point that way but we do know that the person was probably disguised, beard etc. The height too, about six foot. Being able to move a dead weight of forty-seven kilograms needs some strength, suggesting male but we can't rule out..."

"Unless there are two."

"Colin, is there anything else from the body that might determine where he was held?" Cyril asked.

"There were scratch marks to the lower arms." He turned to the screen and brought up the relevant images. "These show that he rubbed against a wooden chair arm. Minute splinters suggest a mahogany wood with traces of, and I hardly dare say it, bee's wax. The seat to which he was strapped was probably Victorian. There was also a severe decubitus ulcer to the sacrum." Another image followed. "It tells us that this person probably never left that seat so it might be a Victorian type commode."

"So you're saying that Tony Thompson was secured to a seat for over three weeks, fed honey and physically and emotionally abused by one, maybe two people of unknown gender?"

"Yes, and has some kind of container close to hand in an isolated place and is heavily into bees. That is where the concentrated police work should focus because the likelihood is he has Carl Granger strapped to that very commode and when he dies and he starts his game of cat find mouse with us, he might also find and trap the next victim."

Cyril looked at the white boards and specifically at the word *INVICTUS*.

"Why is he unconquered? Who has challenged him and why? Why tattoo this permanently? Why the tongue? Who has said what? What has come out of the mouths of fourteen-year-olds? What is he telling us? Everything's been in code so far but somehow this is in plain sight."

***

Autumn 1980

Samuel moved the action man figure across the carpet, making strange noises as if the doll were hovering above the ground. He turned the figure vertically through three hundred and sixty degrees before making a crashing sound, then brought the figure to his face and kissed it.

Ian watched carefully as the child hugged the figure.

"What's he wearing, Sam?" Ian pointed to the cloth draped around the figure.

"It's his dress, Daddy, he was going to the ball like Cinderella but he fell down the stairs."

Ian hung his head. "I'm going to kick the football outside do you want to play?"

Sam shook his head never taking his eyes from the figure. "Don't like football. I have to look after him like mummy looks after me."

Ian went into the kitchen. Jose was peeling potatoes. "He never seems to do anything but play with that bloody doll. He doesn't want to play football, doesn't want to play with the cars just the Action Man figure. What happened to the combat clothes and the gun?"

"They're in his toybox somewhere, why?"

"He was dancing this morning, too. Spends too long with you and your bloody mother, he's getting to be more like a girl."

Jose wiped her hands on her pinny before turning so that he could register the anger on her face. It said everything. "If you put in a few more hours to help with him then maybe he'd gravitate more to you, but you spend all your spare time up to your armpits with that pile of junk you keep in the garage. And whilst we're at it, let's face some truths, you shout too much, you demand his attention... he doesn't like football. Some boys don't. He doesn't want to wrestle with you or box. He likes to play by himself. Just accept that. You bully him. It's probably just a phase he's going through. Besides your mother said you didn't socialise well when you were his age. You were also timid. You were frightened of *Dr Who* and when you went to the pictures to see *Darby O'Gill and the Little People* you wouldn't sleep in your own bed for a week. That didn't make you any less masculine. And what about that shawl you carried until you were eight? Give him a break, Ian... go and maul with your car, leave us both be."

Ian stormed from the kitchen, ensuring the door slammed. Jose hung her head. When she looked up, Samuel was standing looking at her, his head to one side.

"I love you mummy. Sugar and spice and everything nice that's what..." he did not finish.

Jose smiled. "I love you too, Teacake." She had called him Teacake since he was born.

"We don't like daddy, do we dolly?" He turned and went back into the lounge mumbling, "Slugs and snails, slugs and snails..."

Jose watched as he toddled through the door, the doll clutched firmly to his cheek as if in deep conversation. She felt a degree of uneasiness but was unsure as to whether it was Ian's anger or what she had just witnessed, either way, she closed her eyes and wept.

Chapter Thirteen

Stuart finished adding small black crosses to a map of Harrogate and the surrounding area. Every marking signified some form of metal container, each would be circled once it had been checked. He knew from initial enquiries that some had been locked for years considering the overgrown state of their surroundings. These would be visually checked but not opened and the reference filed separately as the time taken to trace owners was considered to be unprofitable.

"What if the one you seek is a hundred yards outside the search zone?"

Stuart turned, the pen between his lips. "Bloody funny that... thanks for that! Now piss off!" He was pleased to see that the facial expression of the young DC changed as he sloped from the room muttering that it was only a joke.

Stuart prioritised any that were near water treatment works or swimming pools. The number to inspect proved daunting and on more than one occasion there had been false hope. The majority were used for legitimate storage but one had been found to contain a small cannabis factory. The general public had been asked to check lock-ups and garages but nothing had been forthcoming.

Liz sat doodling, the phone lodged between her shoulder and ear. It rang a number of times before being answered. The person on the other end said nothing but Liz could hear breathing.

"Hello."

"Hello, can I help you?" Pamela Shepherd asked timidly.

"My name is Liz Graydon and I'm trying to contact Pamela Shepherd."

"I'm Pam Shepherd. How can I help you?"

Liz breathed a sigh of relief. "I'm a police officer looking into an incident that occurred at the Stray Fair and I believe you were working there for a Mr Jenkins."

"Yes, Bruce has been very kind. He gives me work when I'm back at home. I've a commitment to my aunt which means I can't take permanent work."

"Do you recall the youth that went missing during the fair?"

"Ms Graydon, I do remember the reports but if you are going to ask if I saw him or served him, I'm going to have to disappoint you. On such occasions you see so many faces it's impossible to pick one out unless there's something unusual or outstanding about them. You tend to remember the abusive ones but generally it's just another evening and another event."

"I understand, but you do realise that we have to check all avenues? When will you be returning to Hempsthwaite?"

"I nip back briefly whenever I can. I have a dog and I really shouldn't be away like I am but my neighbour is very kind..."

Liz doodled the words *very kind* again on the pad and joined them with circles that had the appearance of spectacles, before scrawling, *why is everyone so kind to Pamela????*

"... Mr Melville, he looks after Sam. I buy the food."

"Will you ring me when you're next over, I just need two minutes of your time. Tell me, did you use to teach?"

"Yes, worked in a private school, taught science but when my mother was taken ill I was under a lot of strain and so I left. I've been a carer ever since, firstly mum and then my aunt. You have to do what you feel is right."

"Thank you. Don't forget to call me when you're next home." Liz gave her number and asked Pamela to read it back. She wanted no excuses for her not making contact.

Liz put the phone down and stared at the doodles. She wrote the word *CHECK!* and underlined it. Turning to the computer she ran a full background search on Pamela Shepherd... something was just not ringing true.

***

DC Henry Jones finished reading the report he had written after interviewing Flight Lieutenant John Simms, Officer Commanding the Air Cadet Squadron that both boys had attended. It noted that although they had been friends, they did not meet socially outside the regular two weekly meetings and even attended different schools. Both boys had been enthusiastic from the outset and were keen to rise through the ranks, both had recently had air experience flights at Linton. He noted that this had been on two separate occasions. They had joined the Cadets in the school Year Eight as rising thirteen-year-olds. Both boys' records were exemplary. DC Jones had also received a full list of other members of the Squadron and their names were now on a dedicated watch list, even the female Cadets. Details of all the adult volunteers at the Squadron were added alongside their Disclosure and Barring Check, a mandatory check when working with children. All seemed up to date. He added the details to the system and attached copies to all relevant team members.

***

There had been a definite change in the mood of the town with the disappearance of the second youth and the discovery of Tony's body. More news coverage brought with it greater supervision from parents. Fewer youngsters were seen at the parks or playing on The Stray. There was no panic or fuss, just a sense of caution that was evident when the schools returned after the summer holiday. Traffic was heavier than normal and around some schools, chaotic, as anxious parents brought or drove their children. For a town that had often been labelled, *the happiest place in the United Kingdom to live*, it was showing subtle signs of strain and Cyril realised that. It was reflected in the televised interview he gave for the local north east news. He felt hamstrung, requesting parents to be vigilant. He felt inept whilst reassuring the general public that the full resources of the North Yorkshire Police Force were working on their behalf.

***

The second week of the new school term fell like a hammer blow to Cyril's team as three new jars of honey were found. Each had been left in a public place, the first on the stone marking the place of the long-demolished Brunswick Station on Trinity Road, the second beneath the CCTV camera stanchion facing the Cenotaph and War Memorial, and the third outside Harrogate's Tourist Information Office. Cyril could not help but feel a flutter in his stomach; three jars, one found on Trinity Road. Was the name of the road significant concerning the placement of the jars? The second one had been found at a site commemorating the dead and the third... He did not want to contemplate the thought of who the next victim might be. Was the murderer planning to kidnap a tourist? It might also be noted that one was right under a CCTV camera. You could, my friends read that as, *right under our bloody noses*, he thought.

The incident room was full. It was wrong to say that there was a degree of optimism but every new piece of evidence found or left meant that the killer could have made an error; it would only need a small trace of DNA, a partial print or a hair. Photographs of the identical jars were displayed on the screen, their labels, immaculately placed, straight and level. The familiar, handwritten style was clearly demonstrated, the only difference being the name. It carried the title, '*Tabulae Rasae Honey,*' the pretension of which did not escape Cyril.

Cyril spoke first. "It's Latin, a rough translation, and I had to look it up," he said before referring to his notes – "*the mind not yet affected by experiences or impressions.*" Cyril paused. "He's bloody playing with us. There's one consolation and that is, Carl may still be alive. There are no tattooed pieces of flesh in the jars only small neatly tied clumps of human hair and they have proven to be Carl's. The honey appears to be the same and therefore we can assume at this stage that it's from one batch. It's no surprise that on the back of the labels we find more marks. This time we have the words *Mercy, Deliverance and Voiceless.* The Forensic handwriting people suggest the words are case sensitive, also written by a left-handed person. It's a reference but as they are all situated in a different area of the label, I'm assuming that this is not to a specific location. You've had time to ruminate on them, anyone want to make a suggestion?"

There was a long pause. A voice from the front table broke the silence.

He crouches, voiceless, in his tomb-like cell,
Forgot of all things save his jailer's hate
That turns the daylight from his iron grate
To make his prison more and more a hell;
For him no coming day or hour shall spell
Deliverance, or bid his soul await
The hand of Mercy at his dungeon gate:
He would not know even though a kingdom fell!
The black night hides his hand before his eyes,
That grim, clenched hand still burning with the sting
Of royal blood; he holds it like a prize,
Waiting the hour when he at last shall fling
The stain in God's face, shrieking as he dies:
"Behold the unconquered arm that slew a king!"

The room fell silent. Nothing was said. Cyril simply stared at DC Brian Palmer who sat his head slightly lowered, looking a little embarrassed and red-faced.

"Sorry, I couldn't help myself."

"Sorry? Don't be. Where the bloody hell did that come from?"

"It's from *The Dungeoned Anarchist* by the poet Charles Hamilton Musgrove. I had to learn it for an elocution examination in a past life, my A.L.C.M, if I remember correctly. My mum wanted rid of my Yorkshire accent, believed I'd get a better job if I could speak properly. Those three words brought back the terror of the exam. I remember it was at The Unity Hall in Halifax, it all came flooding back, made me think of it straight away."

"And are we glad it did! Your mother was right. Please write it on this acetate sheet and thank your mother for me when you see her."

Brian looked up as he was writing. "She's dead."

Cyril blushed a little before placing a hand on Brian's shoulder. "Sorry," he whispered.

Cyril slipped the sheet onto a projector and the poem came up on the screen. He ringed three words then underlined the last line.

"*Invictus* has come back to haunt us yet again, ladies and gentlemen! Owen what do you know about poetry, you surely studied it at school?"

"All, hey nonny, nonny and daffodils, sir. Bloody hated it at school and I'm not too keen now, especially when you see it linked to cases like this. There's one thing though." Owen moved to the front. "Look, references to a *tomb* and a *dungeon*. Are we looking in the wrong place? Aren't they placed underground? Shouldn't we be looking for cellars, drains, old water type tanks, bunkers?"

"Reference too, to a bee maybe, sir? *Clenched hand still burning with the sting,"* someone added.

Cyril took a deep breath put his hands to his face and rubbed his eyes. Was this swift discovery the chink in the conqueror's armour that they so desperately needed? The butterflies bounced in his stomach.

"I want that poem analyzed, all the meanings and possible nuances, I want to know about the poet anything that might just put us a little way ahead of this clever bastard."

Owen looked at Cyril who knew just what Owen was thinking and he nodded. "Check the tunnel, lightning doesn't strike the same place twice but I want it checking and I want it doing immediately."

Owen pointed to an officer. “Get onto the council, go with them and do a full search of the Brunswick Tunnel. I want to know immediately you’ve done a thorough sweep.”

“And Owen, the only other bunker I know of is that on Grove Road but it was converted into classrooms some time back. Check anyway. Also get someone to contact Yorkshire Water, we need a list of obsolete water storage tanks within a thirty-mile radius of Harrogate town centre.” Cyril paused. “Stuart?”

“There are hundreds. Nothing so far from the search of known containers, apart from the discovery of a mini cannabis farm. Six arrests so far so it hasn’t been a total waste of resources. Spoiled someone’s day that did. From all accounts it had been going on for some time. Another two days should see them all cleared.”

Cyril smiled. “Well done!”

“Sir, it may be nothing.” All eyes turned to Liz. “I’ve spoken to Pamela Shepherd, the woman who was assisting one of the vendors at The Stray Fair. She’s at present toing and froing between Harrogate and Ilkley, she’s caring for her aunt. I carried out a full background check and all seems fine.... except she used to be a boy, well actually she officially still is male.”

A number of faces that had been looking elsewhere suddenly looked at her.

“I’m aware that this fact in itself should have nothing to do with anything, how he or she sees herself has nothing to do with the police and it certainly doesn’t make them any more or any less guilty in the eyes of the law. However, call it thinking out loud, intuition... I suppose we’ve all experienced niggling doubts when speaking to witnesses, but there was something.”

“Talk to her again and again, Liz. Talk until you’re happy. And Liz, a full report on when he became a she and how that, if at all, has had an effect on her life.” Liz looked down and unfolded the page containing the doodles. Cyril was right, she really needed to interview Pamela Shepherd face to face.

***

July 1982

If ever there was a defining moment then this was it. It came out of the blue. The day had been beautiful, the sky bluer than a robin's eggs. Jose had wrestled the garden into a semblance of order, the borders were full of flowers and the lawn although not perfect, was as good as it could be considering it was the playground of a child and a dog. The paddling pool sat, an oasis of water in the centre. Samuel and two children from the neighbourhood splashed, shrieked and laughed interspersed with the occasion tears.

She could hear Ian in the garage, the doors ajar to allow air to penetrate. He was tinkering with a Triumph Spitfire that seemed to contain more holes than an MOT would allow.

"It's a filigree," he would protest. "Just needs some TLC!"

The degree of TLC seemed to take up most of his spare time and money. This, in turn, continued to bring friction to their relationship. He had given up trying to influence his son to interact in more manly activities having resigned himself to the hope that this would come in time.

Jose glanced from the kitchen window. The two youngsters in the pool were being watched by Jane, the elder sister of the girl with Samuel. She turned to concentrate on the sandwiches she was preparing for lunch. She called Ian who appeared at the door wiping the oil from his hands.

"I'm famished!" He smiled.

"Sit and I'll get the kids in."

Jose leaned out of the door and noticed that Jane had dried them and they were getting dressed. She could see that Jane was a little flustered but simply waved.

"On our way, Mrs Dixon. Just a minute."

Jose sat next to Ian. "Well, will it be ready before winter comes?"

Ian just raised his shoulders. "Needs a little more work..."

He did not finish the sentence, he simply stared as the children entered the kitchen.

Mary, Jane's sister, entered first, smiling. It took a moment for Jose to register the scene but it eventually dawned, she was wearing Samuel's clothes. Samuel came next wearing Mary's followed by Jane.

"I'm sorry," Jane insisted. "He just wouldn't do anything else."

Samuel moved closer to his mother. "I don't want to be a boy anymore. I want to wear dresses, I want to be a girl and be made of sugar and spice."

He turned as if showing off his dress. "I look lovely don't I mummy?"

Ian remained silent for a moment. It was as if the penny were falling but hitting every obstacle before it came to rest releasing his senses.

"Take them off! Take them off now!" he yelled at his son.

Samuel stopped, his head dropped. He lifted his wet eyes to look at his father and mouthed the word *no*.

"What did you say young man?" By this time Ian was on his feet, his voice filling the room. "What did you say to Daddy?"

Sam screamed, "No!" He turned and ran into the garden.

Mary and Jane clung to each other. Mary was already in tears and Jane was close.

"Go to the garage, Ian. Now! I'll deal with this."

It was a moment in time that would never be forgotten, it would mark a significant crossroads. Two people were about to embark on a pathway that seemed less trodden whilst another would struggle to make sense of his failure.

Chapter Fourteen

Cyril leaned across the bed and found comforting, naked warmth. He lifted his knees and smiled as they docked perfectly with Julie's.

"I love this morning moment," he whispered in her ear.

Her hand moved round and held his outer thigh. She made a contented 'mmmmm' sound as if she were about to say, 'me too.'

The sun shone straight needles of clear white light from the narrow gaps in the Venetian blinds, penetrating the soporific gloom. He could hear the clock tick; time too seemed to be affected by the morning moment and it seemed loud and more alive, another being far off in the room.

He slipped his feet out of bed and sat briefly to steady himself. "Would the lady of the house like tea and toast or does she have to be somewhere?"

"Mmmmm, please." The word *please* seemed to go on forever. She rolled over into the warm, vacated space tucking the pillow round her face, her nose enjoying the lingering smell of Cyril's aftershave.

Cyril smiled as he headed for the kitchen.

Within ten minutes he returned. Placing the tray carefully on the bed he adjusted the pillows to give Julie some support.

"I didn't expect you to call last night." Julie caught the molten butter on the plate as it dripped from the edge of the warm toast.

"I'm struggling or I'm getting too old for this," Cyril confessed. His voice seemed to carry a huge weight.

"What? Too old for sex or do the workings of the female anatomy cause you a degree of confusion?"

Cyril's face cracked into a smile. "Funny, very funny as usual. Nope, I hope I can manage sex to your satisfaction and yes the female form still does project certain questions to which I constantly strive to find practical answers." He paused, his expression taking on a more serious demeanour. "I'm talking about the two kidnapped kids and the fact that we really don't have anything. We have enquiries and leads all over the place but nothing to show apart from a white board of confusion. How can it be so hard to find someone who according to the psych wants to be found?"

"Have you looked under your nose?" Julie wiped her mouth. "That was divine… company wasn't too shabby either!" She giggled before giving Cyril a peck on the cheek. "Thank you."

Cyril did not respond to her answer but what she said had found a mark. He recalled many cases where he had felt as though he could not see the wood for the trees, only to discover that the answers lay away from the woods.

"You've followed up on all of the water treatment plants, both active and closed and the swimming pools? Goodness, with Harrogate once being a world-famous spa town you're not short on springs, spas and watering holes. What about those spas that have been closed for years, those connected to hotels? Are they still checked on a regular basis?"

"We've checked, trust me. The only reason that there's a connection to water treatment is your discovery that the body was cleansed with a substance that killed DNA traces, hydroch…" Cyril did not finish.

"Hypochrorus Acid. Yes, but as I said, there was something special about this one. We're still looking into it. Nothing to date but I have someone checking the patent office to see if it's been registered recently. It's got to be new to the industry but there's a chance it hasn't reached the market yet, maybe still under testing."

"So, how would our boy get hold of such a chemical?" Cyril moved from the bed towards the window and twisted the plastic handle to open the blinds. He looked at The Stray. People were already out walking.

Julie was quick to answer. "How could he get hold of polluted, banned honey? Could work in the industry. Look Cyril, he's clever, but not that clever. It's easy to make up obscure puzzles, to link concepts and ideas. Take the labels, Christ, who'd have guessed that they were co-ordinates made up from numbers derived from the positional letters of the alphabet? Yes, maybe someone who doesn't have a life or a job who can sit down all day in a cardigan, whilst chewing a pencil and work these things out. Once you know the answer, it sounds simple but it could have been anything.

"Cyril, he wants you to feel inadequate, he's making you kick yourself for not solving the puzzle. He wants you to feel as though he's beaten you. That's what he's doing, he's making you look where he isn't and he's making you try too hard. When things get tough, and they do too often these days, I always think of the scene in one of the Indiana Jones movies, can't remember which one. You remember it, the one where the guy comes out dressed from head to toe in black and swivels a bloody big sword in a menacing dance of death. People stand back in awe, afraid of his skills. What does Jones do? He takes out a gun and drops him. He doesn't get drawn into a fight. So much for fancy skills, when push comes to pull they mean nothing and the references to honey?" Julie paused ensuring she had Cyril's full attention. "A morning with Google could have given all of those links. But for me, call it women's intuition, there's something in it but it's not too deep. Now the poems *Invictus* and *The Dungeoned Anarchist,* that's where I'd be looking for motive. You've no doubt got some clever fellow looking into the nuances of every word of every line I imagine."

Cyril turned back to look at Julie who lay on her side, the duvet tucked below her chin. Vapour from his electronic cigarette drifted around his head giving the appearance of a halo. He nodded with a degree of uncertainty. She smiled.

"That's my boy. Trust me, the answers are there for us to find, you'll see my clever, handsome man and we'll find them. Now come back to bed and investigate the finer points of pleasing a woman. You'll get this anatomy exam right if it kills me!" She pulled the duvet over her head and giggled. Cyril thought about asking her a question on transgender but then selfishly thought that this might not be the best moment

***

Carl's eyes focused on the far wall of the space. His buttocks were tender and he tried to shift his weight to alleviate the discomfort. It worked but only briefly. He was sure that the wounds were open and weeping, but there was also some numbness. He could not differentiate between wet and cold. He tried to lift his weight on his elbows for a moment but these too were now sore. An aching weakness streamed through every limb. In the dark his eyes strained to focus again on the far wall, it was the same picture that had stared back at him since his arrival. It was Tony. He was aware of his disappearance but that was all he knew. Maybe he was here, possibly trapped, maybe in another room. He closed his eyes, the familiar wave of nausea crept through his stomach. He could taste the sickly sweetness of the honey. Even when the tears came he could smell them. The knotted cloth around his mouth felt choking. He longed to breathe fresh air, to lick his lips and drink cold water. His eyes felt heavy. He stared at the lines that tracked along his left arm.

The sound of the lock and the moving bolts made Carl sit up straight. He knew what was about to happen and he closed his eyes to protect them from the sudden flood of light that would painfully crack open the darkness.

"How's my boy? You'll be all sweetness and light today, Carl. All innocent. You know I bring with one hand and take with the other." The scalpel slit the binding tape on Carl's wrists and elbows. "Do remember not to upset me when I remove this."

Hands untied the cloth from Carl's mouth and he greedily sucked in air. One hand pushed between his legs and retrieved a bucket. Its contents smelled sweet. A plastic jar of honey was placed in his left hand and Carl quickly retrieved the spoon and began to eat. He looked at the face that watched his.

He was so confused. How could someone smile all the time and yet be so evil?

"Four minutes Carl, that's all."

The figure moved away leaving the door open and the sunlight streaming in. He could feel its warmth, he could hear the birds singing. For a moment he thought he could hear the sound of an aircraft. He craned his head listening for clues as to its make. He was sure it was a Tucano, probably out on a training flight. For a brief moment he was away from this hellhole, he was up with the pilot remembering his flight. The views of the Yorkshire Dales folded out below in all their beauty. For the first time in what had seemed an age, he smiled. The figure returned. His smile disappeared. Carl's arms were just about to be taped again.

"Please, I'm so sore."

A hand pulled Carl to his feet and turned him round. The marks on Carl's buttocks from the edge of the commode seat were red and in places open. The figure moved towards a shelf and returned with a small, black pump-action spray. Carl felt the immediate effect. The sting from the fine fluid made him call out. He then felt a gloved hand rub a sticky substance on the wound.

"The honey will heal it or prevent it from worsening. Not long now. Looking at your eyes I know you'll not be here much longer."

Carl's heart leapt. Was he letting him go?

Once the tape was returned, the scalpel blade ran gently down the arm for about three centimetres. Small ruby globules appeared. Carl watched as his captor leaned over and licked the blood away.

"You're getting sweeter by the day. It'll be soon now, very soon."

A blanket was wrapped around his body and Carl knew what was coming next. His head dropped as the door swung closed. He was again trapped in the darkness.

***

The taxi pulled up outside the Methodist Chapel, Hampswaite. The passenger paid the driver and watched the car pull away. Gravel crunched under his feet as he walked down the drive. He could not fail to notice the weeds that broke through the rough surface, giving a feeling of neglect. It appeared to him that this was a building and not a home. It was in total contrast to the properties on either side. His attention was then drawn to the damaged garage door that still gaped partially open. He would fix that, he thought to himself. The same idea came to him every time he noticed it but then this driveway was paved with good intentions. He noticed the blinds twitch on the front window of the house next door, another occurrence that happened each rare time he came in or left. He instinctively raised a hand to demonstrate that he had seen the movement. He dipped his hand into his pocket and retrieved a key. He could hear the dog behind the door and he whispered a few words before opening it. There was no bark. The dog knew the footsteps and the confirming whisper.

John Melville appeared at his door and then he cautiously leaned round the porch looking across at his neighbour's closing door. He smiled.

***

Liz read the report she had compiled on Pamela and made notes. Pamela Shepherd had apparently been a boy until starting school. There did not seem to be a specific date for this. His birth certificate showed the child to be registered as Samuel Dixon, born to parents Jose and Ian Dixon. Parents separated when Samuel was six. Jose never remarried and was supported by her only sister. Samuel was renamed Pamela Samantha Dixon but then the family reverted to Jose's maiden name of Shepherd. Apparently, Pamela left school when she was fourteen and had been educated at home. Liz checked her qualifications, she had done well in all exams with credible A level results. She enrolled at University College Salford whilst still living at home from '94 until '98, studied Chemistry and

PGCE before teaching part time in Clearmount Private School, Eccleston, Lancashire under the name of Samuel Dixon. She used the name Pamela only when at home or with friends. No police convictions, no driving offences. Liz noted that Pamela had started an application in August 2004 for a Gender Recognition Certificate in order to be legally classified as female, but she had failed to provide all of the necessary details and therefore this was pending. Liz checked through the details one more time just to ensure that she had missed nothing and closed the file. She was going to pay Pamela a visit.

***

John Melville woke on hearing his letterbox snap shut. He checked the bedside clock, it was just after five in the morning. Light crept through the thin curtains, casting the room in a blue hue. He climbed out of bed, curled back the corner of the curtain and squinted through the smallest of gaps. He saw the man leaning on the concrete gatepost at the top of the driveway, a suitcase at his feet. His hand raised and waved instinctively at the twitching curtain, demonstrating to the watcher that he knew of his presence. John Melville smiled. “Cheeky bugger!” he whispered to himself. A car pulled up and he climbed into the rear seat. He turned and looked towards the bedroom window and saw the movement of the corner of a curtain. He had guessed correctly.

John dropped the curtain and slipped on his dressing gown. The envelope was still held by the letterbox, it had not fallen. He slipped a letter opener into the envelope and slit open the top. It contained five twenty-pound notes and a handwritten letter.

Money’s to help with the dog. Please let us know if you need more. Really grateful that you can keep an eye on the place. The word *eye* was underlined twice. *Your continued support is gratefully appreciated. We couldn’t do this without you, John, but we feel sure you know that. Keep watching and keep listening. Your reward will come. xx'*

He read it again and then tucked the money into his dressing-gown pocket before folding the note and sliding it into the kitchen drawer. A smile hovered on his lips. Leaning over he collected the kettle and filled it. He would take the dog out later and check the house.

Chapter Fifteen

Annoyingly, Liz could not get the image of Alan Titchmarsh out of her head as she turned left over the narrow bridge crossing the River Wharfe, the shortest route that would take her to Ilkley. She waited for a gap in the traffic to turn right. Titchmarsh, she had been informed, was one of Ilkley's famous sons. Stuart Park had announced the fact to her the moment she had told him she was going to the town. He had then pulled a lecherous face. Liz did not even have a garden and she could kill the small pots of herbs bought at the supermarket without any assistance from a gardening expert, so Titchmarsh held little attraction, besides, he was twice her age. This combination of ideas brought Sonja James's house to mind and she shivered involuntarily as she remembered the sensation of her shoes sticking to the carpet. The blatant sound of the horn from the car behind brought her to her senses. She had missed three opportunities to pull out from the bridge crossing into the stream of traffic and a frustrated motorist just wanted her to move. Raising her hand in apology she joined the traffic.

Originally, she had planned to just call on Pamela Shepherd unannounced but then Cyril had suggested it would be more professional and less threatening to make an appointment. "Could be construed as victimisation of a minority gender," were his exact words. As usual he was correct. Much to her annoyance, it had taken three days to arrange!

The A69 was busy and the traffic seemed to slow to a standstill as she approached the town's centre. She waited for the mechanical dashboard voice to tell her to turn next left down Little Lane. Her destination was her next right, Nelson Road. Stone terraced houses flanked the road and beyond she could see the railway station and past that, high on the horizon, the famous moor. She tried to put the tune into her head to blank Alan's image.

Liz did not even get a chance to knock. By the time she had closed the gate and taken two steps along the path, the front door opened. Liz had seen a photograph of Pamela but she was taken aback by just how attractive the lady was in the flesh. She hated to think it, but her facial features were so delicate and feminine.

"DS Graydon? Good morning, Pamela Shepherd, how good of you to come all this way." The smile seemed as genuine as the welcome.

Liz followed and was surprised by the cottage's quaint room. It smelled of lavender.

"What shall I call you? I can't keep saying DS Graydon."

"Please, call me Liz for this interview."

"Thank you. Liz, I've organised a neighbour to sit with my aunt for an hour. I thought we might go and get a coffee and have our chat away from the house. It would give me a break and auntie just gets so confused when she hears a stranger's voice. Is that alright?"

Liz felt as though she were losing control of the situation but then resigned herself to the fact that she had nothing on Pamela other than a hunch.

***

Betty's Tea Room was busy but they managed to secure a table by the window looking out onto the car park.

"Now, how may I help?"

Liz went through the details of the case and explained how they were trying to find anything that might give a clue as to the identity of Tony Thompson's murderer.

"I know one thing, Liz, we were very busy. There were two stalls selling the type of food we serve. Gary Barton had a fire, a fridge I think, and he didn't open on the day the kidnap took place. When you spoke on the phone, I checked the dates just to be sure. Bruce runs a good ship, it's immaculate and he's really fussy about following hygiene procedures to the letter. When you're busy that can be difficult. Gary's not bad on the hygiene front either. I know Bruce isn't the most handsome male specimen but he's got a heart of gold. That leaves Sonja! What does one say about her without sounding like a bitch or it appearing to be professional sour grapes? I wouldn't eat her food if I were starving. I guess that tells you everything."

Liz knew that only too well. "So did you work every evening?"

"Look, Liz, I've been dealt a strange hand as I know you're aware, what with mum's illness and death and then my aunt needing round the clock care, I work when I can. Those two people were all I had when I was growing up. They stuck by me, protected me when life was not easy. Growing up kids can be cruel especially when they find that you have an Achilles' heel. My heel was in the open and couldn't be hidden with a metaphorical sock... it was in your face. School for me became unbearable as you can well imagine, so mum decided I should be educated at home. My father couldn't cope with anything but inanimate objects. He loved finding broken things and making them perfect but ironically, he couldn't cope with his fractured child. He didn't have the patience nor the inclination to help make me whole, make me what I wanted to be. He couldn't accept me for what I was. I know he blamed himself."

Liz felt a lump in her throat and sipped some tea. There was, she noted, no sadness in Pam's eyes, just determination.

"My aunt was really good. We'd come here at weekends and for holidays, to people who had never heard of Samuel Dixon. My peer group accepted me here and that was a cotton-thin lifeline that I clung to. Once I'd finished University and my PGCE, I started part-time teaching. Being at Manchester gave me some time away from home, there was greater tolerance and I wasn't alone with my *problem*." She made her fingers sign inverted commas. "Even then in the primitive naïve nineties, a transgender person was not seen by everyone to have climbed out of a UFO, probably due to the likes of Mark Bolan and David Bowie." She laughed at the memory. "And besides, I was older and a lot tougher. I know we females should have soft, delicate skin but I have consciously developed the hide of a pachyderm."

"Pam, I noted that you had applied for a Gender Recognition Certificate but to date you have failed to complete the necessary procedures."

"Look Liz, for the last goodness knows how many years, my hands have been rather tied but I've promised myself it will be submitted one day. I enjoyed the teaching. My mother, who by then had moved to Hampsthwaite with a guy she had met on some dating agency, seemed fine but let's quickly close that chapter. She rented the house, nothing special and they lived together. Strangely enough we all got on well until I found him trying to get into my bed as well as my mother's when I occasionally stayed at the weekend. Funny the way life deals the cards. And before you ask I don't do the lottery." Both laughed and it lightened the mood.

"So when your mother was ill you moved over to Yorkshire?"

"Yes, he soon buggered off when she started to grow worse... Goodness! Look at the time. I really must get back." Pamela stood. "I'm sorry it's all a little rushed but please, come over again it's been so good to chat to someone who doesn't make demands. Maybe we could pop out for some lunch?"

Liz smiled. "That would be lovely," she lied.

***

Cyril was relieved to have a morning away from work, it meant that he could clear his head and try to fill it with the things that did not have a habit of causing angst and stress. After a short walk from home he turned down Albert Street. He had one goal, a destination that would give him the *fix* that had taken over a small part of his life, paintings. The entrance to the auction house was set within a row of shops, estate agent offices and eateries. The entrance was a single black door almost hidden within the simple, commercial façade that stretched the length of the street.

The corridor leading to the main auction rooms was hung with paintings of various sizes; cabinets along the right-hand side held myriad illuminated small sculptures. One by the great Henry Moore drew Cyril's attention. *A cat can look at a king!* he said to himself, knowing full well, after checking the catalogue, that it would sell for over half of his life's savings. His reason for calling in on the first viewing day was to inspect two paintings. One, by Stuart Walton depicted a gritty Bradford industrial street scene and the second, a Lawrence Isherwood oil, was entitled 'Tate Gallery, Blue Rain'. The Walton, although beautiful, was too big for his flat but the Isherwood, well? He looked at the estimate, checked the condition and placed a cross next to it in his catalogue with a figure of £1,400. This would be his limit. He stood back to admire it again when he felt his phone vibrate in his pocket.

"Bennett."

It was Owen. "Sir, we've had another jar handed in. It's gone to Forensics but should be back here this afternoon. I thought you'd like to know."

"Where was it found?" Cyril had rolled up the catalogue and was tapping it against his thigh.

"You'll not believe this but... it was on a garden wall on Robert Street."

Cyril's stomach churned. "I'm on my way in."

***

John Melville opened the front door. The sun's warmth was immediate and he breathed deeply as he took the dog lead from the hook just inside the door before closing up. He squeezed through the end of the hedge that separated the two driveways, a route he always took before putting the key in his neighbour's door. The dog made one deep loud bark.

"Come on fella, you know who it is." There was no further sound.

Once the lead was attached, man and dog crunched their way up the drive and on to Gower Lane. He would be away for about an hour.

***

Owen was leaning against the stone wall outside the police station trying to enjoy some midday sunshine, a mug of what looked like coffee in his hand. He saw Liz pull up in her car and waved. He waited for her to approach. "Had a good day?"

"I'm more bloody confused than ever. Christ, she's a pleasant character, not at all what I was expecting and that fills me with all kinds of concerns."

"Want to chat it through? I'll share my last drop of coffee." Owen gripped her round the shoulder. "A problem shared…"

Liz looked at the mug and her mind flipped back to sticky carpets and dirty fingernails. "Thanks but I just need to let it all…" she looked in the mug and found inspiration, "that's the word I was looking for, ferment, yes, I'll let it ferment for a while. Something might bubble to the surface."

Owen looked at Liz and then into his cup before raising his shoulders. "Speaking of bubbling, we have another jar. With Forensics at the moment but should be couriered back all neatly bagged and on Flash's desk by sometime this afternoon." Owen frowned and pulled a face that suggested fear.

Liz laughed and punched his arm. "Behave!"

***

Cyril dropped the auction house catalogue on his desk and stared at the bagged jar for what seemed like an age. Liz kept looking at Owen but neither spoke.

"What do we have this time?" Cyril sat and inhaled his electronic cigarette. The menthol hitting his mouth seemed to lift his mood.

"No tattooed flesh but…" Owen paused and looked at both colleagues. "It contained a plastic strip one of those Dymo embossed labels. It reads, *You are no closer, you're as hoppless as the boy."*

"*Hoppless* what on earth? Forensics, what do they say?"

Owen just shook his head. "Nothing apart from the finder's prints. Not the same quality of honey, different sized jar; the label just read HONEY. Note it's in block capitals. *The Scribblers* at Forensics completed spectroscopy analysis on the ink and there's no match with the ink used on previous labels. They also confirm that there's evidence to suggest that it was written by a right-handed person!"

"Tell me it's rogue. Who brought it in?"

"A Mrs Kenyon lives three doors up from you. Says she knocked on your door knowing you were a policeman but there was no answer. Thought it was important to get the jar to us straight away after all the news stories and so she handed it in to the office in town. She also said that she'd call on you to see if she'd been at all helpful."

"I know Mrs Kenyon! She suffers from dementia." Cyril placed his face into his hands and sighed. The gesture said everything. "Get someone round and make a thorough search. I'll sort out a warrant. Get in touch with her son, he'll be understanding and probably look around the house with you. Just trust me on this. The press release that mentioned that there were messages held within the jars was a big mistake. I think I said so at the time. I wonder how many more are going to turn up?"

Liz watched Cyril's expression as he talked about his neighbour and she could see the compassion within his frustration. She had been aware of Cyril's kindness from the first day she had moved from Leeds. It was a nurturing that seemed to permeate the whole team. Okay, he would not tolerate inefficient policing at any level and he drove himself hard, but there was this compassion, this understanding that made him special. It was then that she realised that all eyes had turned to her, including Cyril's who stared back at her and smiled.

"You wanted to mention Pamela Shepherd? Are you alright?" Owen asked.

"Yes, yes, I'm fine. Just thinking about Mrs Kenyon and her son. It must be so difficult at times."

"I believe it is as I'm sure your Ms Shepherd would concur."

Liz recovered her composure and went through the details of her meeting.

"So she can give us no help I take it?"

Liz shook her head. "I'm going to see her again though... let's say a woman to woman chat! Should have been in social work. I just feel sure there's something more to her."

"Computers, Owen, Carl's computers. Anything?"

"There are a number of deleted files that involved Tony Thompson and three other boys, all of which are now added to our system for close observation. It appears that they were friendlier away from Cadets than the Air Cadet Commander or whatever his working title is, suggested. One area that seemed to take a large amount of their social time together was an online subscriber site. I believe Carl's father was relieved when he left the screen alone and went to play on The Stray."

"I think it's the same for parents of all teenage kids," Liz chipped in. "They're never parted from their phones. Have you noticed whenever people go to concerts they hold up their phones and watch the performance through a small screen? The band is in front of them but they still watch the world through a bloody screen."

Owen smiled and raised an eyebrow as if to agree. "Here endeth the first lesson."

Cyril smiled at her. "You're preaching to one of the converted here, Liz, but I can't speak for the big fella."

Owen just pulled a face as if to suggest he was innocent of all charges and then continued. "Before I was rudely interrupted... We've interviewed the other lads and it appears that the subscriber site was a flight simulator conflict situation site. They'd each fly their own virtual planes, Second World War aircraft as a squadron or against each other in virtual air battles. Strangely, the only one still registered is Tony Thompson, the others unsubscribed after his disappearance. We're seeking a list of subscribers who interacted with any or all of our boys but that's not easy, for one, these sites are available to subscribers worldwide. What with data protection there are rules that even the law enforcement agencies have limited power to overturn."

"So they're all sitting in the same room?" Cyril asked in all innocence, failing to comprehend fully the genre.

"No, sir. You're playing from your own computer and it works through the Internet in real time."

"Are they Air Cadets, too?"

Owen nodded. "Yes, the two are and a few years older. There's also another player who was a regular when they were using the simulator but as I've said, when we interviewed the other two they were both concerned about this other pilot. They couldn't tell me why but they both felt uncomfortable talking about him or her. Something within his messages didn't ring true."

"So we can't find out who that person might be or where they are in the world?"

"At present, no."

"Maybe these two boys could have been murdered, possibly by someone who interacted with them on the Internet and we can do sod all about it."

"Takes time and the correct procedure and process. It will happen but... Digital Forensics are, let's say, trawling."

Cyril picked up the catalogue. "I want a full briefing in two hours and Owen, I mean full. Everything we have. And Liz, I want a clearer focus on your thoughts on Miss Pamela Shepherd. Obviously, something's causing you to have doubts."

He waved the rolled-up catalogue as if to swat a fly and Liz and Owen left his office.

Cyril looked at the wrapped jar within the transparent plastic bag.

He took a ten-pound note out of his wallet and placed it under a paperweight. "If this isn't to do with Mrs bloody Kenyon, then that tenner goes to charity," he said to himself.

Within the hour Cyril's phone rang.

"Bennett." He listened as his fingers tapped the top of the paperweight. "Another jar found and the correct labelling device. Right bring her in. Don't charge her, just try to get through to her the seriousness of wasting police time and get onto Social Services and Mental Health, she's known to them. Handle this carefully and sensitively." He listened again. "Yes, ensure her son comes too. I'll speak to him and make sure you thank him for his support. She's been sectioned on two previous occasions." He put the phone down and slid the tenner from beneath the paperweight and popped it back in his wallet. "If we could solve them all as easily as that."

He checked his watch, shook it and looked again. He then slipped the electronic cigarette between his lips and inhaled. He would take five minutes before the briefing.

Chapter Sixteen

Carl had been moved for the first and final time to the grubby bed away from the commode. His eyes, only partially open, stared transfixed at some indeterminate object. They rarely blinked. His lips moved, only small involuntary movements, but it appeared as though he were in conversation with the object at which he was staring. The figure moved quickly within the space, collecting various pieces of tattoo equipment and placing them strategically on a small round table near the commode. Carl's naked body twitched, his left arm went into spasm as his legs curled into what appeared to be a foetal position. At the same time a rasping sound was heard as air was quickly drawn in through his tight lips. All went quiet for a moment. The figure stood and rested a gloved hand on Carl's head.

"Shhhh! You can go, Carl. You don't need to stay here any longer. You are sweet enough. You have my permission, it's alright."

The boy seemed to relax and curl up gently tucking his knees even more tightly towards his chest before his final breath escaped in a steady rush. There was a pause, the body fought against death and as if through pure instinct inhaled again. This time it was a shorter, more desperate breath. His upper arm shook slightly and his eyelids fluttered.

"It's alright, Carl, it's alright. You can rest and go. You have my permission. You are no longer bitter you are sweet and beautiful. You can leave me."

Carl's eyes closed again until there was only the narrowest of gaps between the lids. He exhaled gradually, the breath vibrated the vocal chords for the final time creating a faint but audible note that lasted only as long as the expiration. There would be no further movement of the body, only the occasional sound of escaping gases as the internal organs began to contract when it was lifted and returned to the commode. Carl's head lowered involuntarily as his right arm was taped at the elbow and the wrist, palm facing upward, to the chair's arm.

Within three to four hours the chemicals within his muscles would change and the onset of rigor mortis would begin, slowly at first, the eyes, the neck and the jaw would be the initial muscles to be affected. The rest of the body would follow. Within twenty-four hours there would be a total reversal as the body would revert to its flaccid state. It would be then that the work would begin.

"There, you see, you're happier now. I told you so. This is where the fun begins. Tony didn't seem interested too much either but the results were wonderful. You just wait and see."

A foot touched the pedal and the tattoo gun buzzed frenetically as the needle moved fractionally from the gun.

"Like a million bee stings! Another day and we'll be ready, just another day and we can start all over again. Another naughty boy will take your place and I'll then be able to throw you away."

***

Cyril immediately took control of the briefing. "The last jar found is rogue and we need to be aware of that for future reference. The more the public knows about these cases, the greater is the chance of this happening. While I feel it's important that we seek the support of the general public, we also need to guard certain pieces of information. I'm aware that all the press releases have been cleared to date but let's just ensure that what's said away from the station does not lead to leaks and therefore compromise our ability to get this task done. Secondly, we have checked the Brunswick Tunnel and the other tunnels within thirty miles of Harrogate. They're secure."

Cyril left the room briefly, returning accompanied by a gentleman who looked to Owen to be a teacher.

"I should like to introduce a Dr Christian Macauley, Head of Applied Linguistics at Leeds and a qualified psychologist. Today you get two for the price of one." Cyril smiled at his own joke. "He's gone through the poems we've received and is here to express his thoughts and how they might have a bearing on the case. Dr Macauley."

The tall, relatively young man moved to the front and stood next to the interactive screen. His nervous smile broke across his lips.

"Thank you, Cyril. Please call me Christian when it comes to questions but first let me give you my thoughts." He tapped the screen and the poem by Charles Hamilton Musgrove appeared. "I believe you're familiar with this by now and I know you have your own interpretations, but let me give you mine. By no way are they definitive but... Let's leave the title for the minute. First line, *crouches* and *voiceless* tell us that his victims are at his mercy, they are vulnerable and controlled, maybe that is a position that has been reversed from the past. They are victims like he once was." He added the notes around the sides using a tablet. "*Tomb-like cell* gives us a clue as to location. It will be windowless, so yes, shipping container, drain, garage, lock-up, old box van or wagon. This might mean that the perpetrator has the ability to move around. The words *his iron grate* make reference to either steel doors or a draining cover. The second line tells us that the kidnapper has no compassion, only hatred for his captives. *For him no coming day or hour shall spell deliverance or bid his soul await,* reinforces that there is no mercy or reprieve, probably because the kidnapper had similar experiences."

He paused and looked around. A number of officers were adding notes to a copy of the poem.

Pointing to the screen, he continued. "Now if you look at this line, *The black night hides his hand before his eyes*, refers to the darkness the boys find themselves in, a darkness that conceals their perceived evil, that keeps them in the dark, keeps them from their usual evil ways until he can enforce his revenge. I also believe that this could refer to the fact that the victim is hidden in plain view, close to where we are right now. *Waiting the hour when he at last shall fling The stain in God's face, shrieking as he dies*. I think the *shrieking* is not a reference to the victims but to the kidnapper. His perceived mania and sense of omnipotence are clear in the last line where he again refers to *unconquered*." Christian took a drink from the glass on the table. "There's more but can I ask for questions so far?"

"You refer to the perpetrator as male, is that deliberate or is there evidence from the text used to suggest gender?"

"Thanks for bringing that important point up. No, I merely use the term. From the evidence in the written word your kidnapper could be either sex."

"Are the clues given through some self-belief that they'll not be caught, a certain arrogance?"

"It seems to me that this person is giving you a path to follow, so yes, total arrogance. Remember he need give you nothing but I feel he believes himself to now be untouchable, above God."

"Is he or she seeking recognition for a perfect crime or does he want people to see that he's taken his revenge for something that has happened in the past?"

"I'm sorry, but I cannot answer that. What I can do is give you my educated judgement on the reason this text has been sent to you."

"What about the line, *The grim clenched hand still burning with the sting*?"

"Knowing what Cyril has told me, I can assume that this refers to his past frustration at something that brought anger and deep anxiety, possibly clinical depression. The hand closing in on itself and making the fist demonstrates a threat to his way of life. But the sting, I know that someone who dies has experienced death's sting but I feel that might be too simple an explanation. This is only my interpretation again but it could also pay reference to the bee and Royal Jelly. By using honey he is restoring something, maybe his confidence, his old life once the anarchists have been dealt with."

Cyril put his hand in the air to ask a question.

"I think the Chief Inspector needs the loo!" Owen said quietly.

Cyril pulled a face at Owen expecting some sort of jibe. "I shall reward you later, Owen, with a difficult task." Laughs rumbled around the room and some of the tension eased.

"You have a question, Cyril?" Christian asked.

"Why would someone refer to two fourteen-year-old boys from good backgrounds as anarchists?"

"We all know that an anarchist is someone who tries to bring about anarchy, a state of disorder or, and I believe this is one of the keys you are looking for, non-recognition of authority. I know many people observe teenagers fighting against authority whether be it in the home, in school or in the street. Just take the way we've all tried to find our own identity as we travelled through puberty. Fourteen-year-olds... they are simply pushing the boundaries. If someone shows any weakness when working or dealing with kids of this age, they can, in my experience, be totally cruel and selfish. If working in a small group, say in a classroom, they can destroy a teacher's confidence and in some cases a career. Let me bring you back to the passage, *hate*, *no deliverance*. As we've said, revenge."

There was silence as each person looked through his or her notes. Liz particularly related to the reference to teaching.

"And for what it's worth, the tattooing of flesh makes the victory permanent, indelible. The victim is marked for life and some might believe death. The victor is showing that he is unconquered. Invictus."

He collected up his pad and papers. "Just two other thoughts I can leave you with. Firstly, the term *jailer* suggests someone more powerful than just a prison guard, as if he is meting out the punishment without judge and jury. The *sting* signifies the punishment and secondly, a little more abstract in thought but maybe... prison might be a biblical reference... eye for an eye etc. Thank you for listening. Any more questions?"

The room was quiet.

"If you need anything Cyril has my contact details."

Christian left the room and Cyril escorted him into the corridor. They shook hands.

"Don't know if it's been useful, hope you find something in it."

"I'm grateful. Thank you."

Cyril returned to the briefing. "So where do we go from here?"

There was a pause before Liz spoke. "I'm back to Pamela Shepherd, taught fourteen-year-olds, also could have been perceived to be weak owing to his reluctance to conform to, let's say a more male way of dressing. Maybe they picked up on his transgender and just maybe he made that deliberately easy."

"The more we find, Liz, the more I have to agree with your intuition."

"I want vehicle stops, box vans, those with no windows and metal rear doors, all checked. I also want you to investigate any wagon trailers that seem to be popping up as impromptu advertising hoardings in fields next to main roads. Stuart, that's for you. Also you might get the lads to pop around the farms to see if there are any used for yard storage."

Brian Palmer just raised a finger to attract Cyril's attention. "Sir, I've been checking my crime timeline, starting from the first abduction to the release of the jars and then to the second kidnap, followed by the dumping of the body. If Tony were poisoned over a period of time, that time is either up or getting close for Carl. We really need to step up a campaign in schools warning the kids about drinks labelled *Ichor*, or to make sure they think before accepting anything free, no matter how professional the label or how well known the product is to them. I'm also aware, sir, that the more info is in the public domain, the more problems it might bring us from copycats, but it just might prevent another kidnapping which according to this timescale is imminent. Might I suggest community officers visiting schools to speak in school assemblies targeting fourteen-year-olds?"

"Good, yes, thank you. Please organise it."

"Liz, get someone to lead a more thorough check on Pamela Shepherd's history, detailed search on parents and anyone connected to them. I'm curious to know more about her father and also the guy her mother met on the Internet."

"Sir, one other thing." It was Brian Palmer again. "I've Googled the meanings behind all the key names we have to date in this case and interestingly, the name Pamela was created by a Sir Philip Sydney for use in his poem *Arcadia*. He possibly wanted it to mean *All Sweetness* from the Greek word pan meaning *all* and *meli, honey*. I just found the connection with another poem and sweetness and honey significant."

Cyril just looked at Brian and nodded. "The power and the destruction of the Internet demonstrated within thirty minutes. Good Brian, thanks. Add it to the board." Cyril looked at Liz and raised an eyebrow. "Food for thought. I wonder why she chose Pamela?"

"Nectar, sir!"

"Now, grab a coffee and spend some time assimilating the info you've got, check the boards and then double check. You might want to get straight on with your lines of enquiry but we're missing something and I feel sure it's in here somewhere." Cyril slipped his cigarette into his mouth. "Owen!"

Cyril and Owen moved through to his office. "I want some TV coverage for an update organised for tomorrow at the latest. I also want you to pay Carl's father a visit. You have all the details of his computer history with that war subscriber site. See if he knows anything, if Carl mentioned this other pilot whom the others were concerned about. I understand that it will be an uncomfortable situation for you because we've nothing to give him in return, other than we are now working on some new leads."

***

The haunting buzz of the tattoo needle as it penetrated Carl's dead flesh was masked by the rock music that seemed to be squeezed from two small speakers attached to an iPad. The camera situated just over the tattooist's left shoulder caught every movement and tracked the lettering's progress. The inked, stencilled lines could be seen running up the white flesh of the boy's inner arm. Blood had pooled at the bottom of the arm leaving it mottled and purple, a mark that would remain. Any part of the body that was connected with a hard surface demonstrated the same marks. The pathologist would know it as livor mortis or post mortem lividity.

A gloved hand wiped away the excessive ink. "See Carl, that's not too bad all things considered. *From the once strong, now comes the sweetness.* I know, Carl, that it's inaccurate but it will serve its purpose. Tomorrow I'll remove it and serve it in one jar. Now, my beaten young friend, I'll leave you to sleep."

A hand tapped the button that glowed deep blue on the top of the speakers and the room was immediately silent. "Until tomorrow."

***

The television crew set up in the police car park. Cyril checked his appearance in the mirror before shaking his watch he had fifteen minutes. He read through his notes quickly, they had been scrutinised by a Corporate Communications Officer and he had been assured that although it was unusual to go live on kidnap cases, it was essential and he was confident that his brief followed the strict established guidelines. The words *without fear or favour* came into his head; it was something that had been drummed into him when he was dealing with the media. He did not exactly feel nervous just a little self-conscious. It had taken slightly longer for the police press team to arrange the interview than anticipated but better late than never.

Opening the file Owen had left on his desk, Cyril noted that there was nothing from Carl's father other than disappointment; his opinion was that nothing appeared to have been done. Maybe this interview would either demonstrate that there was a thorough and continuing investigation or, to some, an admission that they held no real clues. He straightened his tie and left to face the cameras.

Cyril completed the television interviews and felt the same as he had on previous occasions. It was a sensation of impotence, a feeling that he was purely going through the motions. He had offered the warning regarding children accepting or consuming strange energy drinks. He had advised being accompanied when playing or travelling to and from school. He was also aware of the chaos this would cause with parents suddenly, but rightfully, becoming overprotective. He had explained that more foot patrols would be made available, particularly across The Stray. His parting comments requested that the public remain vigilant and to telephone or email details of anything that was out of the ordinary or suspicious, no matter how trivial they might seem. The incident telephone and email details had been scrolled along the bottom of the screen during the four-minute interview. He knew requests such as these could have a negative effect and that they could be a blessing or a curse.

***

Close-up focusing on the tattoo allowed the camera to capture the moment it was released from Carl's body; it was removed as one piece. Loud rock music contradicted the delicate surgical removal of the sliver of dead flesh, the noise filled the room but the camera captured the whole thing.

"One jar is all we need this time my young friend. They can have the lot in one go. They were no good last time, let's see if they are any the wiser with this, shall we? Sorry, you won't be here to know will you? By that time you should, if they're on the ball, be with them. You'll be home. That's if the police think!"

The figure turned and switched off the camera and then the music. "By tomorrow the police should have this jar and then we wait."

***

Forty-five minutes after the televised interview had been aired, the telephones had not stopped ringing. Every call was logged and detailed and then checked depending on the quality of information. Two calls stood out. Cyril listened to the recordings of the first. It was received from Carl Granger's phone. The voice had been masked using some electronic voice changing software. It was being assessed to see if it was the same voice that was heard on the Tony Thompson video.

"Late again Detective Inspector Bennett. Late again. Funny how the police always fail the innocent."

Cyril played it again. "I take it we'll know shortly from where that call was made from and it will be full of a police presence including a dog?"

"They're on their way. Grove Road Cemetery," replied the officer.

Appropriate I suppose, thought Cyril. "The second call, please?" Cyril listened. Initially the voice sounded tentative and nervous and then, as if the floodgates seemed to open, the words just flowed.

"My name is Samantha Young, I live on Crane Lane. Hopefully, I'm not bothering you but I've been a little concerned since the disappearance of those young boys. There's a farm behind my house that's full of old caravans, the trailer of a wagon and old vans. I just wondered after hearing the reports if there's anything there. It's probably nothing and I don't want to waste your time. Sorry!" The caller spoke quickly with few breaks and the words ran into each other.

"Contact her now and tell her that I'll come and see her right away," Cyril demanded and then waited for the call to be made.

"She's only available after three, works in a school kitchen." The officer held the phone to his ear awaiting Cyril's answer.

"Make an appointment for me to call at four."

Chapter Seventeen

"Sorry, would you repeat that?" Liz made frantic notes. "And when exactly was this? Yes, I fully understand. When can I meet you?" Liz checked her diary, thanked the caller and hung up. Data protection and confidentiality had again raised their heads. She checked Google Earth for directions from Harrogate to Eccleston, Lancashire. Looking at the routes she decided to give the M62 a miss and take a more scenic route. Firstly, she'd clear it with Cyril and then the Lancashire Police. All being well a local PCSO would meet her and attend the interview.

***

The following morning dawned battleship grey and the rain did not improve Liz's mood as she travelled west along the A59. The clouds sat heavily above Kettlesing Head where the field of wind turbines stood like headless Leviathans, their sails appearing briefly at the bottom of each sweep, curling the mist into tiny vortices. Ahead and to the right was RAF Menwith Hill Missile Intercept and Listening Station. There was always something quite sinister about the large spheres that sat trapped behind a nest of razor wire, tall fences and CCTV cameras. Albino dinosaur eggs from a bygone cold era were laid incongruously amongst England's green and pleasant land. Their menace materialised as they grew larger through a veil of mist and spray. She smiled at the disturbing thought that should there be an enemy missile strike, then this spot and all of Harrogate, would be one of the first targeted and the search for a killer and kidnapper would mean nothing. "All a matter of world perspective," she whispered to herself as she looked into the rear-view mirror.

The weather improved as she crossed the Bolton Bridge and by Clitheroe the sun was again shining. Her mood lifted with the brightness and by Eccleston she was buzzing.

After collecting the local officer, he directed Liz to Clearmount School, a large stone mansion of a building surrounded by gardens and sports fields. Liz and the PCSO entered through the main door once the door locking mechanism was released. An elegant, lady in her middle years, greeted them.

"Detective Sergeant Graydon?"

"Mrs Hackworth?" Liz noted the smile. "Good morning, I believe you know Colin, your local Support Officer?"

The Head teacher smiled again and nodded before she shook his hand. "Please."

Liz followed the Head into her office. "Firstly, may I offer you refreshment?"

"Coffee would be welcome. Thank you."

The head made a call. "Now, how may I assist?"

The interview took longer than expected and by the time Liz had dropped the Officer at Coppull Police Station, a building that comprised no more than a pair of semi-detached houses with a small flat roofed office attached to the front, the traffic had started to build as she headed north back to Harrogate. The conflicting evidence tumbled in her mind as the information gleaned from two different sources for the incident set alarm bells ringing.

***

Cyril pressed the doorbell and waited patiently for someone to answer the door. Hearing the immediate, short sharp bark of a small dog he guessed it to be a poodle. He was wrong. Within minutes he had become best of friends with a Shih Tzu, not his favourite breed. He waited to witness the slow accumulation of dog hairs on his dark trousers.

His concern was detected. "They don't shed, Inspector Bennett. I've always had this breed because my children were allergic to dog fur. She has hair."

Cyril was already flustered. The lady spoke quickly, hardly taking a breath, just as she had done on the phone and he was having difficulty in getting a word into the conversation.

He had to raise a hand before she stopped chattering. "Derelict vehicles, Mrs Young. You have some concerns?"

Cyril soon found himself standing in a stranger's bedroom, looking through lace curtains at a muddy field and a farm that appeared no more organised than a derelict scrap yard. His phone rang.

"Excuse me... Bennett." It was Liz.

"Sir, I've just finished talking to the Head teacher at the school where Pamela taught. I need to see you later but I'm still in Lancashire. Could we meet for a drink?"

"My place Liz, Pizza and a good red, you obviously need it. Can you make seven?" Cyril noticed Mrs Young glance across and then look away. He put the phone into his pocket and smiled. "Girlfriends!" He noticed her sharp look of disapproval and he smiled to himself.

"See, there and there and to the right of that building. There's even a box, I've been told it's an old industrial refrigeration unit. It's just behind the unsightly pile of car tyres, Sindi-lou and I see it when we go out for a walk, don't we my little precious? I actually carry her in a basket, it's far too dirty for her delicate little toes. Besides, he has two large dogs and one never knows, does one? We don't take chances do we my precious one?"

Whilst the final words were addressed to the dog and spoken as if to a two-year-old, Cyril let them travel over his head. He took out his phone, fascinated by the farm view. He set the phone to 'movie' and panned round through 180 degrees.

"Who owns the farm and land, Mrs Young?"

"Farmer named Gregson, a horrid individual, lives and farms near Nidd Park. They check this dump every couple of days and as you can see, store any crap they like right behind my house. I've complained to the council on many occasions for all the good it does!"

Cyril, initially shocked by the sudden use of the word *crap*, now picked up the hidden agenda. "You said there were a couple of dogs," Cyril quizzed whilst still looking through the window.

"That's what I've heard but I've never seen them other than when someone's there. As I say, if I'm in the garden we'll see people checking the place, won't we darling." She lifted the dog up to her face and kissed it. "Probably looking for more space to drop another tyre, a caravan or a few tons of dung. It's disgraceful don't you agree, Inspector?"

Cyril muttered something about it not being the best view he had observed, but he did not want to be quoted in the next epistle to the council.

***

Cyril arrived back and went straight to the command room.

"As much as you can find about this address, also chase up the owner and any details we have on them. It's urgent. Check with Stuart and see if that farm and this building have been inspected yet. I want a meeting on site within twenty-four hours, otherwise it's a warrant, not that I need one." Cyril afforded himself a smile; such authority came with his rank!

***

18.55, the late sun reflected from the window of one of the houses opposite and cast a golden glow into Cyril's lounge. He sat, a glass of red wine on the coffee table, an auction house catalogue on his knee and Stevie Winwood playing on the stereo. He inhaled his e-cigarette, watching the light change in the room as the sun set even lower. It was five past seven when the doorbell broke his trance.

"Sorry I'm late, needed a shower, what a day! Grim start but it just got better and better until coming over Blubberhouses. Wagon decided to avoid a corner and in doing so removed a whole stone wall and a tree. As you can imagine there was something of a delay. I recognised one of the traffic lads so managed to push my way through a little more quickly. Must be one of the only perks of this job, that and getting dinner prepared by your boss!" She smiled. "Anyway just realised that it's your gym night isn't it?" She pulled a face as if to show an apology.

Cyril nodded. "Yes, but I'm fighting a strong Yorkshire instinct… you know that dreadful feeling when you've paid your membership fee and you're not using it. The emotion builds up inside giving a dreadful and painful ache, not muscular but it certainly hurts just as much. The pain is here… he tapped his right buttock, it's deep in my wallet. Third missed session so that's twenty-five quid!" He smiled. "I'm throwing cash away like a man with no arms!"

They both laughed.

"Walking?" Cyril asked as he collected the bottle and a glass.

"Oh, yes and do I need this!"

Liz settled into a chair and sipped her wine. "Right, here goes! As you know Pamela Shepherd was born Samuel Dixon. He stayed a Samuel through school right through university and at the start of his teaching career, but by that time he was known as Pamela Shepherd when not at work. Complicated, I know but understandable."

She took a longer sip of wine leaving only a drop in the glass. Cyril obliged and topped it up.

"Thanks. However, as you can imagine, Sam believed he was the wrong sex and was transgender. She told me that she would have successfully applied for a Gender Recognition Certificate had it not been for her mother's illness. She had started the application."

"So Pamela was not the teacher, Samuel was?"

"Yes, I'm glad you're keeping up because I wasn't at first. You could imagine the difficulty, an unofficial name change would have been impossible as the police checks, compulsory for working with kids, would have caused so many complications. He knew this when he was training so was prepared. The logical process for Samuel was to train and work as a male and live as a female. I'm sure it's not impossible, difficult and emotionally damaging but not impossible. But…"

Cyril moved to the edge of his seat. "But?"

"Originally Samuel was teaching chemistry full time. His mother moved to Hampsthwaite to be with this guy she'd met using a dating agency and all seemed well. As a new teacher, Sam appears to have had some discipline issues but the Head assured me that they were resolved. Most young teachers find it difficult developing the correct relationship balance, some try to be too friendly and it all goes pear shaped." She sipped more wine. "This is where it becomes a bit hazy and although the dates are clear from her employment record, it's difficult to track in a way. Sam had some time off, initially the odd day but then a week and then longer. Unofficially, the Head told me that Sam was suffering from depression but she let slip that one of Samuel's students had seen him in Manchester one Saturday, not as he knew him but as Pamela. This rumour went round the school. Kids can be cruel and little things began to happen. A handbag appeared on Samuel's desk, knickers were tied to his car, kid's stuff. What's more interesting is that I've seen photographs of both Pamela and Samuel and you would not be able to identify one as the other unless you were, let's say, up close and personal. Seeing Sam leave in a morning and sitting with Pamela in the evening, then you would. The Head believes that it wasn't one of the boys who identified Sam but it was one of the parents who'd possibly bumped into Pamela and after a conversation put two and two together. The child obviously overheard a private parental exchange they shouldn't have and one thing led to another."

An alarm sounded in the kitchen.

"Hungry?"

Liz nodded.

"Tell me the rest over dinner."

Cyril brought the pizza and salad and all was quiet as Liz started to eat.

"I'm starving!" She picked up a slice and between mouthfuls continued. "The school went through an Inspection, you know, these formal judgements public services have to endure."

Cyril nodded.

"Well, his teaching was seen to be unsatisfactory, mainly because of his lack of class control. There was nothing riotous, kids weren't hanging out of the windows or throwing things but the report clearly makes reference to an atmosphere of fear and anxiety within lessons."

Cyril looked puzzled. "Who was afraid and anxious?"

"This is the thing, it was the teacher who displayed these emotions. The report stated that on two occasions certain boys seemed to dominate the lesson. There was a feeling of intimidation and rewards were given frequently by the teacher to maintain order. It doesn't state what those rewards might have been. I'm aware that some people go to pieces in those formal, monitoring situations but the Head believes it was something more insidious. It was the week after this Inspection that one of the pupils made the allegations."

Cyril picked a tomato from the salad bowl. "Am I ahead of you? There was an accusation of sexual impropriety maybe even bribery?"

Liz paused before nodding. "There was a suggestion that he'd grabbed a boy's groin on more than one occasion and also that he'd gone into the changing room after football and watched him shower. The Head and the Deputy interviewed Samuel and of course he denied it all. There was no evidence to suggest he had been in the shower area, even the supervising member of staff supports that. Regardless, he was suspended on full pay pending further enquiries. You can imagine for a teacher who was already hovering on the edge of a precipice, it wouldn't take much to send him over."

"The boy making the accusations, how old was he?"

"Fourteen, but it wasn't just one boy, four boys corroborated the original accusation."

"Conspiratorial. Let's stick together and that way we make the shit stick. What happened to them?" Cyril picked another tomato.

"Parents were brought in and you can imagine the mess. When it was decided to involve the police, two boys withdrew their allegations and suggested that the others were lying too. They were both suspended for three days. It should have been longer but the Head believed that their honesty should be taken into consideration."

"So the police were involved?"

"No, the parents of the other two only wanted their boys to be taught by another teacher. As you can imagine, even though the Head should have brought in the police as bullying is a two-way street, she played the safe card. Let's say she got what she really wanted and that was rid of Mr Dixon. She was probably more concerned about saving the school's reputation by keeping it out of the press. After all, weak teachers are expendable, school reputations take time to build. You wouldn't want to throw away your good name over some transvestite who failed to make the grade as a teacher would you? Then again you could say she was looking after the boys' best interests."

Cyril was not convinced but said nothing on the matter. He had worked with inept coppers who had eventually, with the correct support, made the grade. "Come and sit over in the lounge and I'll open another bottle. So what happened?"

"Samuel didn't return. He had sick notes giving him nearly a year away and then he resigned, never returned to the school or any other as far as his records show. The Head paid him a visit on three occasions during his sick leave, it was part of a support philosophy the school had put in place but only paid lip service to. Each time she turned up at his flat she met his girlfriend. Strangely she referred to Pamela as a lovely caring girlfriend! He was never there." Liz looked straight at Cyril awaiting the response and it came quickly.

Cyril choked on his wine; a fine red mist of ruby droplets sprayed the catalogue on the coffee table before he took control of his breathing. Tears came to his eyes.

"If she couldn't tell Sam and Pam were the same person, how did some parent identify him from a brief encounter in Manchester?"

"Unless it wasn't a brief encounter," Cyril suggested, recovering his composure and wiping up the wine. "Boyfriend? Another man who wants to be a woman. One who has a high-powered job and a family? Meets with like-minded people on the third Saturday of every month when he's supposed to be at work? Who knows? Do you have the names of the two boys who wouldn't retract?"

"Running a check as we sit here." Liz looked at Cyril and could almost interpret his thought processes. "Thanks, Cyril for the meal and the ear."

"It's nothing. Got me out of the gym. You do know what that means?" It was meant as a rhetorical question because he was going to tell her whether she knew or not. "We have at the moment one, possibly two dead fourteen-year-olds, same age as the boys who destroyed Samuel and his teaching career. We have clues that suggest that the kidnappings are retaliation for something that occurred in the past. We have evidence to suggest that the person committing the crimes has a sound knowledge of chemistry and we have someone with a connection to Harrogate. Most importantly, Liz, we have someone who believes that they're unconquered, that they've risen above it all and their life is now on an even keel. Believe me, that's the worrying part because we don't know what else of which he or she is capable."

"As far as Pamela is concerned, that's only circumstantial and it's wafer-thin. All we can do now is talk to her. I need to confront her. If she's been living in Ilkley for the last few months, then that could put her out of the frame. I'm seeing her again and I have a lot more questions in my armoury than before. I also want more details on the chap her mother lived with. What we should remember is that this is all lovely and cosy. It all points in one direction and in my short career that's not the way this usually works."

Cyril's phone rang. "Bennett." He listened. "Contents? Please get someone to bring me round details and photographs and make sure the jar's couriered to Forensics immediately. Yes, here and as soon as."

He looked at Liz who felt suddenly uncomfortable. She shivered a little. "I need a strong coffee and suggest you do too. We have another jar and this one looks genuine."

Chapter Eighteen

The last rays of the September day's sun were almost horizontal, making progress to the west blindingly difficult. Pedalling hard with his head down and straining against the incline of Penny Pot Lane, Christopher was not only knackered, he was late. He had promised to be home twenty minutes ago but the ride had taken longer than he had anticipated; it was a school day too.

Ever since the Tour de France had streaked through Yorkshire he had been hooked. He had even added his old bike, once he had daubed it with yellow gloss paint, to the many that were enthusiastically displayed along the Tour route. Christmas brought a new carbon racing cycle and brightly coloured Lycra matching that worn by his hero, Sir Bradley Wiggins. His aunt added a pair of yellow, reflective glasses and then there was a top of the range helmet. Even with the best cycling gear, he was finding the hill unusually difficult until he realised that the rear tyre was slowly deflating. He swore. It would be another half an hour at least now. His mum would be frantic.

He pulled into the edge of the road. He would ring her and then repair the puncture. He slowed more quickly than he had anticipated; his shoe did not unclip from the pedal as fast as it should have and to make matters worse, he was craning his head to look at the flat tyre; consequently he fell sideways onto the road. It was more embarrassing than painful but he felt his phone, held in a pouch on the back of his jacket, crash against the tarmac. He wrestled to unclip the other toe before scurrying from under the bike. *It's only flat at the bottom* he could hear his friend's jest the last time this had happened. It brought a smile to his face. He took no notice of the white van travelling in the opposite direction but the driver instinctively touched the brakes momentarily after seeing the bicycle fall sideways towards the centre of the road. She carried on a short distance before pulling up. The driver looked into the side mirror and watched the silhouetted cyclist move his bicycle off the road and onto a dirt track before disappearing from view.

Christopher pushed the bike up the gravelled incline away from the road; he was safe here, not that there was a lot of traffic. He checked his watch determined to test how long it would take to strip and replace the inner tube.

The van reversed into a farm driveway. The driver checked for traffic before heading back up the lane into the blinding low light. The trees to either side hid the small turnings that sat at right angles to the road and as the driver approached the track where the cyclist had fallen, she slowed before turning. There was a slight incline and the van accelerated, the wheels spinning on the loose gravel. For Christopher, he was taken unawares and turned to see the van approach; he simply stared as the front of the van hit his precious bike before colliding with his legs, the impact bowling him over. The driver was braking hard causing the van to slide to a halt. The cycle quickly became trapped under the front of the vehicle, its own front wheel spinning in slow protest.

"I'm so very sorry, I lost control. I didn't expect you here. I thought you'd be off the track. I saw you fall off and wondered if you needed help. Are you hurt?"

Christopher sat up and looked as the stranger smiled. "I think I'm fine." He ran his hands down his legs. "No, my shorts are torn and just look at my bike! Look at my bike!" He pulled out his mobile phone from the pocket at the back of his jacket. His eyes looked at the stranger. "The glass on my phone's broken too but I think I did that when I fell in the road." He tried to dial home but to no avail.

"Where do you live? I'll take you home and sort out the damage with your parents or we can get you an ambulance and I can take your bike home. It's up to you. I'm so very sorry."

Christopher looked at the blood on his grazed knees, then his phone and his bike. He peered into the face of the woman staring at him. "Could you take me home, please? I feel a bit dizzy and I'm already late."

The driver helped Christopher into the van and loaded the bicycle into the back. "Where to young man?"

"I live in Darley, do you know it?"

The driver smiled. "Put on your seat belt otherwise we're going nowhere. How old are you, Christopher?"

***

Cyril looked at the photographs attached to the new whiteboard that sat on an easel in his room. He understood the meaning of the tattooed flesh immediately. He also ascertained from the DNA tests that it had been removed from Carl's body post mortem. He was pretty sure that he could predict the exact day that they would discover his corpse. He gazed at the evidence and the clues stared back. This time there was nothing hidden, it was, as the good Dr Macauley had identified from the poem, in plain sight.

From the once strong, now comes the sweetness.

Cyril read it out loud.

"That's nearly the same, sir, as what's written on the Lyle's Golden Syrup tin. Read it this morning as I was eating my porridge. *Out of the strong came forth sweetness*. It's printed under a sleeping lion. Fancy you mentioning something so similar. Spooky that."

"Do you know where it's from? By the way the lion is definitely not sleeping, Owen."

"Trick question? Well seeing it's getting late, yes, I know where it's from I've just told you, the syrup tin."

Cyril refused to be drawn; he could almost see the smirk on Owen's lips. "It's from Samson's Riddle, a biblical narrative where Samson sets a riddle for the thirty Philistine wedding guests to solve.

Out of the one who eats came something to eat
Out of the strong came something sweet.

"Do you know the story?" Cyril asked in all seriousness but neither Liz nor Owen answered. "No? I'm going to give you a condensed version and I want you to jot down any words you might think are relevant to the case."

Liz brought Owen a pad and pencil and they sat at Cyril's desk.

"Firstly, the story is from Judges 14:14." They both scribbled. "The riddle is based upon a private experience. He killed the lion on his journey and on returning he saw bees had made a hive in the carcass." He looked at Owen and smiled. "The lion was definitely not sleeping. He asked the thirty Philistine men at his wedding feast, he was marrying a Philistine bride, what the riddle meant." Cyril tapped the riddle written on the board. "If they solved this they would receive thirty pieces of clothing and if not, they would pay him the same. The wedding feast would last the usual seven days and that was the time Samson gave them to solve the riddle. On the fourth day they were no closer to an answer so they threatened Samson's bride with violence and ridicule if she didn't tell them. She didn't know the answer, but fearing the threats, she begged Samson to tell only her, suggesting that he didn't love her if he kept a secret from her. Each day she begged and each day she wept when he refused. He eventually relented on the seventh day and she then told the Philistines who were members of her own family. They came to Samson. *What is sweeter than honey? What is stronger than a lion?* As you can guess, Samson was furious and left his new wife as she had deceived him and returned to his own family. Afterwards he killed thirty Philistines and gave their clothing in payment of the lost wager."

Liz and Owen read what each had written and started to look for similarities. Cyril watched. There was a knock on the door. They all turned, it was Stuart Park.

"We have another missing youth. Should have been home at six, mother waited until now."

Cyril checked his watch, shook it at looked again. "That's only an hour."

***

After a short drive, the white van turned down past Menwith Hill listening station and indicated to turn right onto Main Street.

"It's that house on the left, the one with the lights on top of the gateposts." Christopher smiled and waited for the car to slow. He looked up the drive and saw the front door open and his mother run down towards the van.

Christopher opened the van door and walked towards her, his head lowered. He was expecting her to shout but she just hugged him. The driver went to the rear of the van and retrieved the bike and his helmet.

"I was so worried, what's happened to you?" His mother ran her hands down his legs feeling the torn material and seeing the blood.

"I didn't unclip my toe from the pedal and fell into the road. I had a puncture. This kind lady brought me home. I've broken my phone too."

His father was already down by the van and was collecting the damaged bicycle.

"Thanks very much, a good Samaritan." He smiled at her. "I'm Christopher's dad and you?"

"I'm Rory's mum." She smiled hoping that he would see the joke. It took a few moments and then he laughed.

"Sorry, Matthew, Matthew Birks."

"Penny Rogers. I saw Christopher fall off his bike on Penny Pot Lane so I returned to help him, although far from helping I nearly ran your young man over. That's why the bike's worse than it should be."

"Don't worry about that, I'm just so grateful he's safe. What with the two missing youngsters..."

As he spoke a police car, its blue lights flashing, pulled up behind the van.

"Shit, we should have told the police he's safe. Excuse me please, Penny."

Matthew, looking a little red faced, handed her back the cycle and approached the two officers. Within fifteen minutes a call had gone into the station and both the van and the police car were heading towards Harrogate.

***

Cyril, Liz and Owen returned to his office, each carrying a coffee. Owen hated false alarms.

"So, what did you glean from the story?"

"*Judges* the word could be relevant, who judges? 14:14... two boys both fourteen years old and this riddle appears after the second child has been murdered." Owen was the first to comment but then Liz, who in Cyril's mind was the deeper thinker, had picked up on the term *private experience.*

"If a riddle is set using purely private experiences then it becomes almost impossible to solve." Cyril could hear Julie's words and he smiled inwardly. "It can only be interpreted that's all. It made me think of the numbers we encountered on the first set of jars, they meant something to the writer. It was contrived and private but meant bugger all to anyone else, to quote Owen here. You had to realise that they were relevant to a location. Had someone given that clue and had someone betrayed the killer and handed us the jars in sequence, then maybe we'd have discovered the meaning and we would have been waiting at the co-ordinates for him to arrive. The only way Samson's riddle was resolved was by betrayal, threat and treason. So was our kidnapper and killer a Samson? Has someone so close to him betrayed him and for that he has, like Samson, taken revenge?"

"There's the reference again to honey," Owen chipped in. "*Out of the strong.* Does this mean that at one time the boys, the fourteen-year-old boys held all the aces, they were the stronger, they were in fact bullies, but in the end they were sweet, they had been transformed. Is that the reason for this honey business? What about the term Philistine? We used it at school a lot. Is it suggested here as a derogatory term for the police?"

Cyril raised an eyebrow at Owen's vocabulary, he was impressed, "And the seven days? What of that?" Cyril looked at them both after noting down their comments on the whiteboard.

Neither spoke. Liz looked down at her notes. "He doesn't hope to kill thirty does he, sir or does he plan on bringing the walls of the temple down on himself in an act of self-sacrifice?"

Cyril looked at Liz. She had known the story all along but had said nothing to save exposure of Owen's biblical ignorance. Smiling at her he shook his head before turning to look at Owen. Owen pulled a face like a child poses when confronted with a difficult question and determined to appear engaged.

"Don't strain yourself, Owen, as it's conjecture. Could it mean that the body will turn up in seven days or will it be the eighth, as Samson delivered the dead men's clothes on the eighth?"

Cyril looked at his watch, turned and wrote the date 21st September on the board. "If anyone wants a wager?" He paused but neither spoke. "Think I just heard the bell, it's home time for you good people."

Owen looked at Liz and mouthed the letters P… U… B. She nodded in agreement. It had been a strange day.

As they left his office Cyril called, "Owen, farm visit tomorrow, early, 7.30 here. Bring your wellington boots. Liz, when do you see Pamela again?"

"Monday, sir. Tomorrow I'm visiting her house near Harrogate… just a feeling."

Chapter Nineteen

A light autumnal mist loitered around the agricultural buildings at the upper end of the drive. There was a seasonal chill to the morning. Owen stood to the left of the farm driveway, his tall, bulky frame leaning against the low stone wall. He stared at his mobile phone. Wearing a tired blue, waxed cotton jacket and dark trousers tucked into incredibly clean wellington boots, he neither seemed like a farmer nor a police officer. Cyril looked him up and down.

"Very smart, Owen," he observed as a cloud of vapour was exhaled from his nostrils. A syrup of sarcasm dripped from his shallow smile. "Those are cleaner than your shoes." He pointed to the boots with his electronic cigarette.

"Didn't want to let the side down, sir, hours they took, bloody hours. Hands will never be the same again. More than can be said for yours, sir. We must be morphing into each other." His gaze did not shift from the small screen.

"Touché, Owen."

Owen smiled.

Three uniformed officers had arrived at the same time and were looking towards the buildings. A van transporting a police dog pulled onto the grass. Cyril strolled down and spoke to the officer who remained in the van. All that was missing was the landowner. Cyril noticed Mrs Young looking through the raised net curtains of the bungalow and his heart sank. When she saw Cyril look towards her she waved. Cyril nodded but averted his eyes quickly, relieved to see a Range Rover turn into the driveway. It came to an abrupt halt trapping the dog handler in his van. Cyril waved the driver to pull forward.

A tall man climbed out. He was in his mid-sixties, smartly dressed, a checked flat cap added to his farming credentials. Cyril noticed the two dogs in the back of the vehicle.

Turning his collar up, the farmer announced his arrival and annoyance at being called to attend a meeting on his own property.

"Who's Bennett?" His manner was as direct as a Yorkshire man could be for ten minutes to eight in the morning.

"I'm DCI Cyril Bennett and you are?"

"Let's cut the crap, Bennett, I've a farm to run. You know who I am, you bloody well ordered me here remember? Now then what is it that interests you about my private property? It's probably that nosy bitch over there grumbling and bloody moaning again. It's a working bloody farm not *Emmerdale*. She expects all year spring lambs and bloody daffodils." He turned his head and looked towards the bungalow, his action resulting in a sudden drop in the net curtain.

After an explanation and threats that a warrant could easily be acquired, the farmer reluctantly followed Cyril and Owen, who in turn followed the Police dog and handler, at some distance, towards the dilapidated buildings.

"I'm surprised, sir, that your farms were not inspected earlier."

The farmer just grunted.

"The dog is using the scent of something we're trying to trace so if what we're searching for is here or has been here recently, he'll find it. Are all the containers unlocked?"

"They all hold stuff we use on the farm so they're locked. The keys are here." He tapped the pocket of his coat.

The dogs in the back of the Range Rover barked their anger at having to remain locked up but whilst the police dog was working, Cyril had insisted that they remain in the car, much to the farmer's annoyance.

The police dog worked its way around the various pieces of machinery and parked vehicles, occasionally doubling back to have a second look. It continued until arriving at the cold store that was positioned on two steel trestles. The dog moved more slowly before sitting in front of the double doors. The handler stroked the dog and it gave a short bark but remained still. The handler tipped his head towards the container.

"It might be something, it's the most active he's been but don't get your hopes up, he's not really enthusiastic, sir."

The farmer frowned. "There's nowt in this. It's not been opened for ages."

"Do you have the keys?" Owen requested. He already resented his arrogance.

He threw the keys to Owen who checked the two locks and pushed in the key. It would not turn.

"Wrong key!" Owen gave the farmer a look that would unnerve a front row rugby forward, before tossing the keys back at him with deliberate force that made him miss the catch.

"Them's right ones." He retrieved them from the grass. "Can I check 'em?"

Owen moved his hand as if to say, *after you, Claude*.

The farmer fumbled with the key each time attempting to turn it in the lock. He increased the force and looked round with a puzzled expression. Removing more keys from his jacket he checked the label attached to each one. He shook his head.

"Shit! These should open this. These locks look newer than I remember. Give us a minute."

He took out his mobile and dialled. There was a pause. "Cold store keys. Have you changed the bloody locks?" There was a silence. "Why? What the bloody hell for and why didn't you tell me you dozy sod? Get your arse here now with the bloody keys and be sharp!"

The farmer's face was red, not from embarrassment, but from anger. "He can do bugger all that lad o' mine. Needs a firm kick up the bloody arse for wasting my bloody time."

"And mine," added Owen. "Why was the lock changed?"

"He said that when he came a couple of weeks ago someone had put a different lock on the door, only a cheap one so he says he cut it off and he put these on. He's bringing the keys, he'll be five minutes. Do you want to check everywhere else?"

"Now why would someone do that?" Cyril enquired, a look of total innocence etched on his face. "Well?"

"How the bloody hell do I know, it's news to me. You'd better ask that son of mine when he arrives."

Owen gave Cyril a knowing look. He organised a uniformed officer to stand by the door of the cold store whilst the others checked the caravans and the other containers. Most held junk metal and pieces of obsolete farm machinery.

"If you don't lock stuff away the Tinkers will nick it. Trust me, I know and your lot does bugger all to help once it's gone. Just look at the number of church roofs that have lost their lead."

Owen put his hand to his head and just stared at him. For once words failed him.

A motorbike splashed through the few puddles and pulled up next to the farmer who swiftly swatted the rider on the side of the helmet before holding out his hand. The rider passed over two keys. "That's from me. They want a word."

Cyril smiled as the farmer handed two keys to Owen, he had learned one lesson at least that morning. Owen walked round the police dog; it waited patiently, the slow, metronomic wag of its tail brushing the dirt aside, but there was little from its general demeanour to suggest that anything would be found. Owen slipped the key into the lock and the first sprang open, he then did the same with the second. He turned to look at the dog handler.

***

Liz parked a little higher than Hampsthwaite Chapel. She looked down the road, it was quiet for that time in the morning. All she really wanted to do was look around the outside of Pamela's house. If John Melville, the bloody neighbourhood spy, were true to his word he would be about to walk the dog. She needed just to wait and watch. She looked at the dashboard clock. 08.22, she was prepared to wait until 09.00. Her stomach rumbled. Lifting some tinfoil from her bag she unwrapped a piece of cold toast.

At 08.31 she saw the dog appear at the top of the drive quickly followed by John Melville who reined in the lead. He checked for traffic. Liz instinctively lowered herself into the seat hoping that he would not notice her. Her heart sank as he turned up towards the car. Dropping her toast onto the passenger seat she turned the key and moved away from the kerb before indicating to turn right down Hollins Close. She kept the car running and watched the end of the road through the rear-view mirror. The dog crossed the road followed again by Melville, his arm outstretched giving the impression that the dog had full control. *Strange for an ex Police dog handler,* she thought. Cautiously she waited for a few minutes and then headed back to the main road. John Melville was disappearing round the corner. With luck he would be away for at least thirty minutes.

Parking by the Chapel she quickly crossed the road. The familiar crunch of gravel on this occasion disturbed no one. The garage door yawned. Moving quickly down the side of the house she peered into the darkness. She flicked the torch on her phone and the disorder quickly became apparent. A sudden movement from a dark recess caused her to jump backwards. A feral cat bolted for the door. There was nothing else of interest that she could see.

The back of the house was as untidy as the front; the remains of a once organised, partitioned garden was just visible beneath the rampant summer growth. A trellis was held drunkenly vertical by the strength of a climbing rose. Ivy clung to the garage side its spidery, inquisitive fingers delved rudely under the wooden bargeboards and then spread onto the corrugated asbestos roofing. She turned and looked at the house windows and then at the roof. A small garden had sprouted in the gutter. Liz moved towards the downstairs windows. The kitchen seemed surprisingly orderly, so too was the lounge apart from a few dead flies and bluebottles that had expired on the dusty sills. It was then that she felt uneasy, a sensation that caused the hairs on her neck to tingle and to feel as though they were standing. She sensed someone or something was watching her. She had seen nothing other than the cat but the feeling was intense. Stepping back she looked to the bedroom windows again. One of the curtains did not seem the same, as if it had been moved slightly at the corner from when she had first glanced at the windows, but then on closer inspection, she was not sure. She stared at each frame for a few seconds trying to penetrate the inner darkness. There was nothing.

Moving to the front of the house, she knocked on the door as loudly as possible and listened. Again nothing. She moved to the front window, all seemed in order. Even the upstairs curtains still had the limp left corner, they had not moved since her last visit.

She returned to the rear of the property once more and stood in the centre of the garden, looking again at each window. The sensation returned, she again felt invisible eyes. She turned to look at the garage window that was partially covered by the ivy and grime, it was only then that she realised where the observer was.

***

Owen moved towards the cold store door and the farmer stepped to one side. The dog stood in anticipation its head craning forward. Cyril noticed the electric cable strung across from the main building on a catenary wire.

"Is there power to this?" Cyril asked before Owen twisted the handle to release the mechanism that locked the top and bottom of the metal door.

The farmer pointed to his son. "Lights, put 'em on."

"Open, Owen and let the dog in first as soon as we have light." Cyril nodded to the handler.

The door swung open and the dog entered followed by its handler. Owen watched from the door. The dog worked its way round before climbing on boxes and plastic drums. It sat then barked. The handler moved and looked behind a steel barrel.

"Sir, there's some clothing."

"Bring the dog out. Owen, close the door and lock it then ring for Forensics." Cyril pointed to two of the uniformed officers.

“Nobody comes near. I want one of you by the door please and one at the bottom of the driveway.”

He turned to the farmer and his son. I need you both at the station this morning for fingerprints and DNA samples. I require a few more answers, particularly from you.” Cyril pointed to the son. “And if you say one word…” he then pointed to the farmer, “the Detective Sergeant here will caution you and arrest you this very minute.”

Owen smiled and moved forward.

“I’ll drop the dogs home and we’ll come right away. Do I need a lawyer?”

“No, we need finger prints and DNA and some answers to eliminate you from our enquiries… it’s called co-operation, Mr Gregson, if that word is at all part of your vocabulary.” Cyril realised that he had used the farmer’s name for the first time since his rude introduction. He must be slipping.

***

Liz slowly turned and looked at the rear of the garage. She jumped backwards. The wide-open eyes returned her gaze staring through the breach in the ivy. The skin appeared unnaturally pale and dirty, the head, bald. She looked more closely once her heart rate had returned to near normal and then she smiled. She felt so foolish she let out a laugh and she stepped towards the voyeur before quickly moving away the tendrils of ivy that held it upright. The limbless mannequin stared blankly, the eyelashes on one eye were the only traces of hair. It fell backwards, no longer supported by the tendrils then even they vanished. She smiled again.

“What do you bloody well want?” a voice boomed loudly from just behind her.

Liz jumped again for the third time. “Shit!” she squealed, stepping away from the trapped, prostrate, plastic torso. Her eyes focused on the man standing yards away.

“Mr Melville you very nearly gave me a bloody heart attack.”

The man's facial expression did not change. "So what do you want?"

Liz slipped her hand into her jacket and brought out her ID. "We've met before, Mr Melville, we spoke about Pamela."

He did not look at the ID just stared straight at her.

Chapter Twenty

Cyril looked at Owen as Mr Gregson and his son left. "Father knows nothing but the son... How old would you say he is, Owen?"

"Could be anything from late thirties to late forties. Looks as though he's had a rough life. Father's a bully and an arrogant git. I could have smacked him on more that one occasion, the bastard."

Cyril smiled. "I'd pay money to see that, Owen."

Within the hour the tests had been completed and Jason Gregson was sitting in front of Owen, whilst in another interview room Cyril faced his father.

"Does your father often hit you in public, Mr Gregson or was that chastisement we witnessed a one off?"

Jason sat, his head down. He first shook his head and then nodded. "He's always like it, has to show he's boss. Doesn't beat me like he used to, Christ as a kid I was black and bloody blue."

"Any particular misdemeanour?" Cyril asked, but seeing the quizzical, vacant look on the man's face, he simplified the question. "Why?"

"You name it, he'd belt me for it."

"What's usually kept in the cold store?"

"It should be junk but I put stuff in that I don't want him to see or know about. He rarely goes in. Checks the place but doesn't take the keys, just walks round the area with the dogs. If there's owt to drop off or collect then that's my job. He had a bit of a thing for the woman who lives in the bungalow a while back, used to get his cocoa there regularly he said until they fell out."

"When was that?"

"He's always falling out with women, treats them like cattle. They have to be there when he says so, always wants his own way. Fell out with her a couple of months ago. Now she gets her own back by complaining to the Council. Does the old man's head in."

"How many lady friends has he had?"

"Christ loads, ever since mother left."

"So when did he meet Mrs Young?"

Jason looked puzzled. "Didn't meet her in that sense, she's a tenant."

***

Liz began to control her breathing and smiled before moving towards John Melville. "Where's Sam?"

"Why are you here? You know she's away. Do you have a warrant to come snooping?"

Liz was taken aback, she neither liked his aggressive attitude nor his rudeness. "I'll tell you what I'll do shall I? I'll go back to the station and get a warrant to search this property here and also..." She turned to Melville's house. "... this one. Seems to me that people who are so defensive and aggressive have something to hide."

John Melville smiled and folded his arms. "That's bloody true love we have something to hide and it's called liberty and privacy. Now if you coppers think you're above the laws of this land then please be my guest but Christ, girl, as some actor said... *make my day.* I can assure you there'll be trouble. Now leave before I call the police, you're trespassing."

Liz glanced up the drive and two people were looking back towards them.

"Are you alright, John? Do you want us to call the police?"

"You were seen, Neighbourhood Watch, it's a wonderful thing. They contacted me."

"I think she's just about to leave but thank you." He waved to the couple.

Liz turned and walked up the drive. The dog barked from behind the closed front door. Her face was red as she passed the two spectators and her blood was boiling.

***

Cyril looked at Gregson. "What's with your lad? He seems to me to be lacking in confidence and a degree of common sense."

"Aye and do I bloody well know it, that's why he's still at home, nobody 'll have him. Bloody useless at school apart that is, from getting into trouble. His mother used to despair but she left ages ago."

"Why was that?"

"Caught me with another woman. Christ, we always had people working the farm and usually one thing led to another. You know what it's like."

Cyril made no comment. The pause encouraged Donald Gregson to continue.

"All he seems to do now is maul on the bloody computer and for a man of his age it's probably porn he surfing if that's the right term."

"Is your son forty-three Mr Gregson?" Cyril received a confirming nod. "Is he in a relationship, has he ever been married?"

"Married? Bloody hell, he can't look after himself let alone a woman on a permanent basis. Always thought that good for nothing lad of mine might be bent, homosexual like, but he goes out with women. What he does with 'em, apart from spend money, I don't know. Maybe that's why he looks at the Internet so much... gives him a clue like." He laughed but received no response.

Cyril changed the subject. "When was the last time you opened the cold store?"

Gregson raised his eyebrows. "Maybe twelve months. That's Jason's job, or one of them. He tends to use it most. I didn't even notice that the locks had been changed when I was there a week back as nowt up there is new… mainly old junk but thought nowt of it."

"So, the clothing?"

"Never seen it before, didn't see it today for that matter Inspector. I'll have to take your word that it was found. I couldn't have told you what's in half of the containers up there. I've a better idea now."

"I'll be five minutes. I'll get someone to drop in a coffee."

"Two sugars and a biscuit would be perfect."

Cyril tapped on the door to interview suite three and entered. "A word."

Owen came outside.

"Get him a coffee. I want to swap round, you know the drill." Cyril copied Owen's notes and read them whilst Owen took Cyril's.

Within five minutes Cyril entered and studied Jason whilst Owen took great delight in visiting Donald Gregson.

"Jason, your father tells me that you like the Internet and that you probably view pornography." It was the casual way that Cyril introduced the subject as his opening gambit that shocked Jason.

"There he goes again." Jason looked straight ahead. There was an element of defiance in his stare that surprised Cyril. "To say he's my father… he knows nothing about me."

"Are you in a relationship at the moment, Jason?"

"What has that got to do with anything?" He looked into the coffee cup. "At this minute no. Do you know how hard it is meeting women when you're my age and work the hours I do?"

"When did you last visit the cold store?"

"About two weeks ago, it was then I noticed that the locks had been changed. Someone had put cheap locks on the doors. The old ones were knackered so it wasn't difficult to remove them, they were more for show than anything. I thought it were yobs as they'd made what looked like a den, made like a bed. Noticed cig ends, some booze bottles, probably nicked and outside were a couple of used condoms. Could have been youths using it for sex and drugs and booze."

"Do you use it for that purpose, a place of your own?" Cyril did not take his eyes from Jason's face.

"No and I don't like what you're suggesting."

"The kids, is that where the clothes came from do you think?"

Jason just lifted his shoulders. "I just tipped the stuff over the barrel and cleaned their rubbish before getting two new locks."

***

Owen stared at Donald Gregson for what seemed like minutes. "You're a bit of a bully from all accounts, I witnessed that when your son arrived on the motorbike. Bullied him when he failed at school, not happy with the way he works, belittle him. Goodness the man's forty-three... when are you going to leave him be?" Owen did not wait for a reply. "What's all this with Mrs Young?"

"Jesus what else has the daft sod been spouting about? She's just a past acquaintance, rents one of my farm properties that's all."

"She's not too happy though at the moment. Put her rent up have we?"

"Right, you either charge me for God only knows what or I'm off! You've had your fun but now I feel as though I've co-operated enough. So what's it to be?"

"You are free to go for the time being. We know where you are if we need to see you after the Forensic results come through."

Owen turned and nodded to the officer by the door.

"And my lad?"

"Your lad, Mr Gregson, is old enough to know when he wants to leave. We'll be in touch." Owen did not lift his head.

Gregson pushed the chair as if in protest, making it slide across the floor.

"Next time I'll have some legal representation you can be assured of that."

"Next time you might need it," Owen growled.

Cyril looked through his notes. “Forensics are testing the clothing and searching the store right now and we’ll have results soon. How many properties does your father own?”

“Five that have tenants, I guess that’s what you’re referring to.”

Cyril waited hoping that he would say where they were and it did not take long. Jason seemed to abhor a conversational vacuum. “He has Mrs Young’s bungalow obviously, two houses in Hampsthwaite, a cottage on the farm and one just outside Ripley, but to be honest that’s a bit of a dump.”

“Mr Gregson, you’ve been most helpful and we appreciate your co-operation. As soon as we know anything we’ll be in touch.” Cyril stretched out his arm and shook Jason’s hand.

“If I can help, I will.” Jason Gregson seemed more relaxed as he left the station.

“Thank you. There is one thing. I’d like one of our technicians to take a look at your computer.” Cyril smiled as if he were asking for a favour.

Jason blushed. “Why? When?”

“Routine when accusations are made. I’ll get one of the guys to take you home and he can do it there or bring it in, your choice, Jason, your choice.”

“Yes, fine.”

Cyril watched as the technician left with Jason and smiled before joining Owen. Liz stormed through the door.

“Fuck!” She threw her bag onto a chair.

Owen looked at Cyril. “Must be that time of the month!”

Chapter Twenty-One

"Forensics have a definite match on a sweater that was found in the cold store. It's a strand of hair, definitely Carl's but it comes from a sweater belonging to one of the lads who was playing football with Carl the day he went missing. He's been interviewed and he admits to breaking into the cold store. He was drinking and he was with a girl and another lad. Parents have gone ballistic so he'll be grounded for ever which is tough." Cyril smiled. "Doesn't get any worse if you're an Air Cadet! He's adamant that it's the sweater he wore on the day Carl disappeared. SOCOs also believe that there was some kind of camera attachment on one wall, possibly battery powered, most definitely light sensitive. I want that kept quiet for now, I don't want Jason deleting all his computer files just yet."

"The sweater hasn't been washed? Christ it's weeks since that football game!" Liz stood amazed pulling a face that showed total disgust.

"Owen's suit hasn't been cleaned for years."

Owen nodded.

"Just don't ask about his ties! They carry a government health warning on the tag at the back!"

Owen just pulled a face, totally oblivious.

"So are the Gregsons telling the truth?"

"We'll see."

Cyril then pointed to the boards around the incident room.

"What address do you have for Pamela Shepherd?"

"Gower Road, number nine."

"It belongs to Gregson as does number seven. You mentioned that her mother met someone through a dating agency. Do you have a name?"

Liz grabbed the file. "She moved into rented accommodation with the guy… Christ, I've not noted the name.

I'm seeing her Monday, sir. A Mr John Melville who's the eyes and ears of the bloody world and an over aggressive bastard, occupies the other house. Should be known as Menwith Hill 2."

"Owen, pay him a visit and take Stuart with you. Before you go do a full check. Liz mentioned that he was in the police… Bradford?" He looked at Liz for confirmation.

"Police dog handler he said."

As they moved away, Cyril checked all the lines of enquiry. The school warnings were running to schedule and the extra patrols were in effect. The only positive was that there were no missing person reports.

***

Cyril was just crossing The Stray when his phone rang. It was Owen.

"Our man Melville tells lies."

Cyril found a bench and sat.

"Wasn't in the force, he was a bus driver, and surprise, surprise, he's the brother-in-law of our friend Donald Gregson. Came to live up here when he, shall we say, took early retirement, which should read alleged violence towards a drunken member of the public, who wouldn't leave his bus one Saturday night. Never been married. Gregson met Pamela's mother through some dating agency and she moved in to one of his houses. Donald spent quite some time there which must have pissed Melville off, knowing that his sister had been badly done by years before. She'd buggered off by then. Now lives in Leeds."

"Melville still remains in the house owned by the guy who did that? Why did he tell Liz he was in the force?"

"He said it sounds better when he, and I quote, *confronts vandals and yobs*."

"What? Who does he think he is, someone from a Marvel comic? Besides, where the heck does he confront vandals and yobs in Hampsthwaite? Doesn't exactly buzz at the weekend does it? When Liz has seen Pamela we'll interview

Gregson again. Dig further into our new best friend, Melville, too. Thanks."

***

Cyril made a coffee, checked his computer and addressed a file marked *urgent*. It contained the details of the two boys who had made accusations of impropriety against Samuel Dixon in 1999. Cyril noted the remarks of the interviewing officers as he flicked through it. The main instigator, now thirty-three years of age, completed his schooling before attending Oxford University and achieving a first in Chemistry. Dr Adrian Smyth had done well academically if not morally. BSC PHD CCHEM FRSC qualifications were attached to his name. Cyril Googled FRSC. It appeared that Dr Smyth not only had five years of experience in his field, he had also made an outstanding contribution to the advancement of Chemical Science. He plotted the time scale… he had been busy! He noted that he was a director of a consultancy specialising in water purification. It was then that a small bell rang in his head. He quickly read through the details of the other student who had died of cancer five years previously. He also noted that Dr Smyth's parents had split up shortly after the allegations at the school had been made. His parents' separation had neither affected his schooling nor his higher education. Mother was still living near Clitheroe, father, Dr Brewster Smyth with identical qualifications to those of his son, had moved to Manchester. No further information was forthcoming.

Cyril looked at his coffee, it was now cold. A white halo contrasted with the dark surface. As a consolation he slipped the electronic cigarette from his top pocket. He felt mentally drained but suddenly he felt that there was light; the steady piecing together of evidence was beginning to drop pieces into place, the border to the metaphorical jigsaw was being joined. He remembered his mother's saying. *It was like getting knowledge from riddled soot*! He smiled.

Pamela Shepherd was definitely an enigma and therefore she had to be a possible suspect. On the other hand, there was only tenuous evidence to keep her in the frame. The farmer, Gregson, was too in your face to be guilty of kidnap and murder but his son? He was a hidden quantity and Cyril's gut told him that there was more to be squeezed from him; the computer, with luck, would shed some light there, but as for being a murderer, he would bet his life savings that was a long shot. There had to be something else something that had slipped inconveniently through the fine net. He knew it would be on the white boards or within the computer files and that it would be so obvious it would be camouflaged. It was like the coded message they had first encountered on the jars' labels, clear, identifiable but so personal that it made no sense to the casual observer. Closing the file, he picked up the telephone. He needed to speak with a certain member of the Smyth family.

Owen burst into his office. "We have another missing youth! Been away now for three hours. Mother received a call to say he was ten minutes away from home but he never showed.

Cyril put the phone down as his stomach churned. "You're with me to visit the family." He stood before requesting that an appointment be made with Dr Smyth. He also wanted an officer to speak with his ex-wife and then he would deal with the son. Slipping the file into a drawer, he left with Owen.

Confronting the parents of the missing child would be even more difficult. So far all he had to show for hundreds of hours of police time was one body and two missing fourteen-year-olds, possibly a third. He glanced at the address and read the child's details. Reading and being a passenger in a fast-moving car did not suit Cyril as he began to feel queasy. He recalled Owen's green complexion after his flight from Nice that time and he closed the file stifling a yawn. He began to perspire.

"What do we have?"

"You okay, sir?"

Cyril nodded and opened the window. "Slow down a little."

Owen glanced across and noted the beads of sweat on Cyril's temple. "Lad was out playing, rang to say he was nearly home and then nothing. We've put out a local news alert but no results have come back yet. Mother's given a description of clothing and we've issued a photograph. She tells us that he's always reliable, never stays out later than he's told as he'd be grounded. She's a one-parent family, sir, two other kids, one older daughter and one younger lad. I've sent a WPC round and contacted Support. They should be there now."

Owen turned onto the council estate and stopped outside number forty-six. Cyril glanced at the three cars parked outside. A few people stood by the gate, obviously journalists. It never took them long. They both avoided the questions but the photographs were inevitable.

The WPC opened the door. "She's holding up well, sir, she's in the back."

Cyril moved down the hall and into the kitchen. The mother had two hands round a mug of tea. A child was on either side of her. The daughter smiled.

The WPC introduced them. Mrs Clegg just looked up. No smile crossed her lips, but a glimpse of optimism flashed in her eyes before being quickly extinguished as she noted Cyril's expression.

"I'm sorry to hear your lad's not arrived..." He was stopped immediately.

"His name, his name's Alan after his granddad." She looked defiantly at Cyril. "I guess you've come to tell me you're doing everything you can to find him when you couldn't bloody well find the others. Christ, what do the police do all day? I saw you on the telly saying you'd put more patrols out and children were being warned at school and the police were doing everything possible, but so far what have you got apart from a dead child?"

The younger boy moved closer to his mother and she smoothed his hair.

"Where was Alan when he rang you? We're checking mobile phone records. Soon we'll be able to pinpoint the place but do you know?"

"I've no idea, ten minutes he said, he was coming back from his granddad's allotment. Often goes to help. Shy lad our Alan."

"Does he always go and return on his own?"

"Its just across Skipton Road, it's all built up, there's no empty wasteland and he's fourteen. They used to be working at that age. I'm not wrapping my kids in cotton wool because you lot can't do your bloody job."

"Where's his granddad now?"

"He's out looking. He went back to the allotment and then said he'd check every route to here."

"How did Alan sound when he made the call?"

Mrs Clegg pulled a face. "Normal, I think. A little out of breath as if he'd been running."

"You're sure it was Alan?"

"Would you like a cup of tea?"

Cyril turned to look at the daughter holding up the kettle, oblivious to her mother's rant.

"No, no thank you but that was kind of you to ask."

Mrs Clegg looked puzzled. "Now you've said that, he did sound different."

"Mrs Clegg, does Alan have a computer?"

"He's got an electronic tablet that the kids share."

"May we take it to see if he's been communicating with people on the Internet?"

"Paul, get the policeman Alan's electronic tablet."

He reluctantly left his mother and retrieved the tablet from the other room.

"Was Alan in the Air Cadets?" Cyril asked looking at the tablet. "Does this have a password?"

The boy shook his head.

"No, he's not getting involved in any military youth organisation."

Cyril glanced at Owen. “The WPC will stay until she’s relieved. Someone will remain here until we’ve made further enquiries. Thank you for your co-operation. We’re trying very hard to trace your lad, you have my assurance on that.”

Owen’s phone rang.

“Last call from your son’s mobile shows him to be near Oak Beck, that’s more than any ten minutes away. I’ve alerted traffic and CCTV coverage is being checked.”

Cyril knew that if he were in a car and the phone was now turned off, tracking was impossible. “I’ll return this as soon as possible.” He held up the iPad.

Cyril rang Liz. “Give Pamela a call at the address in Ilkley and see if she’s there and use her house number not her mobile. Owen, call Gregson and find out where he and Jason are. Organise a call on Melville. If we can place them all it will help.”

Cyril moved from the kitchen into the hallway as Owen made the calls. “Gregson’s at the farm, son’s sitting with our technician.”

Cyril’s phone rang. “Melville’s at home.”

Liz then called to inform Cyril that Pamela was out shopping and that the carer had taken the call. Pamela had been gone for twenty minutes and would return Liz’s call.

“Our Alan’s not with any of them then!”

Cyril stopped by the front door and spoke to the WPC.

“When the grandfather returns take a statement, time Alan left etc. and then ring it through. Thanks. It could be a long evening.”

Liz put on her jacket and was about to leave when her phone rang.

“Is that Liz? It’s Pamela. I believe you’ve been trying to contact me urgently?”

Liz checked the caller’s details but no number was stored.

“Yes, thanks. Are you back at home?”

“The carer has just gone but gave me the message.”

"Is it possible that we could meet tomorrow? Monday may be difficult."

"Goodness thought it was life or death. Just a tick." There was a pause. "Yes, shall we say twelve? I'll book something local."

Liz hung up and then contacted Communications to request details of the last incoming call to her phone. Within ten minutes she had the information. The call had been made from a mobile. She dialled Pamela's home number but there was no answer. She checked Coms again, redialled this time requesting a positional fix for the mobile call. The number was co-ordinated to the area of Pamela's aunt's home. She dialled the home number again. There was still no answer.

Chapter Twenty-Two

Liz knocked on Cyril's door.

"Are you OK?" Cyril asked. He could see from her facial expression that she was troubled.

She explained the situation regarding the calls.

"There's possibly a reasonable explanation, she may have turned the ring tone down for her aunt's sake. If you're unsure, pay a visit but if you do take a DC with you. You might be interested in the latest information regarding Dr Brewster Smyth, father of the lad who made the accusations against Samuel Dixon. Well, two years ago he sold his chemical business in Manchester for six and a half million quid and has now set up a new charitable foundation after lodging a patent for a stabilized cleansing solution. Apparently it's his invention so he's established a factory producing the chemical and all profits go to the foundation."

"That's magnanimous of him," Liz responded, not really taking in too much as she was more concerned as to the whereabouts of Pamela Shepherd. She noted the look on Cyril's face.

"It might be the mysterious product that was used for cleansing the body, we'll see. The pathologist is making the necessary enquiries. When you go over, dig as deeply as you can. Mention Smyth and get the story. If she's innocent it should all come out."

Liz stood. "I'll call when we've seen her."

Cyril's phone rang. "Bennett." He listened. "So nothing incriminating but he liked his porn. Father was right then. Thanks."

"Report on Jason Gregson's computer. Father said he was into Internet porn and it appears he was right. No kids or animals involved, just enjoyed looking rather than doing." Cyril raised his eyebrows.

***

Liz pulled up outside Pamela's aunt's house.

"Let's hope she's in." She smiled at DC Price who had drawn the short straw to accompany her.

Liz knocked on the door and waited. The DC checked for curtain movement but there was none. Liz knocked again. Within seconds she heard the lock turning and a man appeared at the door.

"Liz, this is a surprise, I thought we were meeting tomorrow."

"Samuel! Is that you Pamela?"

The man smiled. "Got it in one. Come in, come in. This must come as a bit of a shock."

The room still held the familiar scent of lavender.

"Tea, coffee?" Sam perched on the edge of the sofa.

Liz stared at Samuel. She found it hard to comprehend fully. He was more masculine than she imagined possible after meeting Pamela. It was probably the hair and the clothing. He even carried himself in a different manner.

"Do you find it strange, Liz? You're not on your own, so do I. Tea or coffee?"

"No, thanks. Just some answers to some questions. Firstly, why Samuel?"

"I was meeting someone who doesn't know Pamela exists and I occasionally dress like this for my aunt. She thinks that Samuel is my brother. It's confusing but I've learned to cope with it."

"You mentioned at our last visit that everyone from Ilkley knew you as Pamela, have things…"

A voice from upstairs broke the conversation. "Is that you Sam?"

"Yes Auntie, I'll be up shortly."

"Is Pamela with you? I can hear talking."

"Yes." There was a pause and Samuel crossed his fingers. "Not really a lie is it! Sorry you were saying."

"So, your aunt believes you to be two people?"

"She does now but it's only been a recent development." Samuel smiled.

Liz looked him in the eye and wondered how Samuel had suddenly become another person in her life. She moved on determined to discuss the fact in the next briefing.

"I paid a visit to Clearmount School as you are part of our enquiry, as you know. The accusations made by your pupils must have been traumatising for you as a young teacher."

"It's a long time ago, it's all in the past. Even if the allegations had never been made, I would be doing what I'm doing now... caring, let's say it's become my calling. Being Samuel was a necessary evil but it served a purpose at the time. As I said to you before, my mother and my aunt were the ones who protected me, who truly loved me when everything was against me. There have been others too who have given me support, been kind and understanding."

"Why did you not involve the police if you knew the accusations were false?"

"Because, Liz, they would all think that the lady protested too much, you know the saying? Young teacher having a few discipline problems, teaching spoiled brats. Makes an interesting equation. Initially four boys made the claims against me but that quickly changed to just two. You probably know that they both withdrew their statements and suggested that the other two were lying. Besides, the Head had made it very clear when she interviewed me off the record that the school's reputation was paramount. That meeting suggested that there was only going to be one outcome. I also had to protect someone else."

"Someone else? Allegedly one of the boys, Adrian Smyth, saw you as Pamela when he was in Manchester."

Samuel laughed. "As I said I had to protect someone else. The dear Head teacher didn't know Pamela and myself apart; she thought Pamela was my girlfriend. Goodness I had some fun with that cow when she called round during my illness. A Mr Smyth did see me in Manchester but it wasn't Adrian it was his father Brewster. I hadn't a clue who he was when we met. I was in a bar known for its certain clientele when he offered me a drink. We met a few times. He knew my gender and I knew what he wanted; he was older, he was rich and it was fun."

"Did you have sexual relations with him?"

"Goodness yes. He would book hotel rooms, always signed himself as Dr Smith. Funny that, no one batted an eyelid! We spent some weekends away. I think he was having difficulties at home. It was after a couple of weekends that I realised who he was when he was talking about his son. Strangely, the knowledge gave me a confidence boost in the classroom, I held a secret over the lad. When we were away for one weekend he heard me chatting on the phone. I used my surname Shepherd, not Dixon; he put two and two together. I guess during one of the many arguments at home I was mentioned and Adrian overheard the conversation. Bingo! Within forty-eight hours the rumours started, the knickers etc. The rest you know. Nothing went on with the boys, there was no touching, the shower allegations they were all bollocks but I had two choices, I either fought it or I pulled away. The Smyth marriage didn't last, it was shaky before he propositioned me."

"So what happened then?"

"I was off work. Brewster was kind and made sure I was OK financially. We met on the odd occasion but I could tell that with the break-up of his marriage, he'd lost a degree of enthusiasm for our relationship." Samuel seemed quite sad as he spoke. "I'm pleased to say our friendship continued. He was always apologetic that's probably why he ensured that the police weren't involved, he probably influenced the other parent too. It was a move engineered partly out of self-preservation but also he wanted to protect me."

"Are you still in contact with him?"

"We chat on the phone occasionally but we seldom see each other. He rarely saw me as Samuel once I'd left the teaching profession. He was kind and compassionate especially when I was looking after mum in Hampsthwaite. He had a business contact in Harrogate who managed to give me some work; the food van. He'd asked Bruce Jenkins to trial some type of sanitizer that he'd invented. Jenkins was an absolute stickler for hygiene. I believe I told you that when we discussed it last time. That's why he wouldn't employ just anybody. Everything had to be done to the letter, floors and equipment cleaned thoroughly. He made sure we sprayed our hands regularly, even pointed to the sprays when his customers bought food."

"Smyth got you the job?"

"In a roundabout way, yes. Initially it was on a trial basis. His wife used to work with him but she developed back problems… it stopped her from performing physical tasks."

"Did Jenkins know about your past?"

"Yes, we used to discuss it during the quiet times. I don't think Brewster said anything to him about the school and the accusations made by the boys, but I told him everything. He got really annoyed. I used to tell him to calm down, that it didn't matter, that it was history. I even suggested that had it not happened, we would never have met. I often used to say that *every cloud…* when he grew cross. He was very protective."

"I'm sorry to be personal but how close was your relationship with Bruce Jenkins?

"His wife wasn't very, what shall we say, accommodating, what with her bad back. Let's put it this way, we were kind to each other." He smiled.

"Sam, I need you." The voice from upstairs broke the short silence.

"I must pop up and see to her needs, sorry."

"No, it's time we left. Thank you for being so frank."

"I take it we're not meeting tomorrow now?"

Liz just shook her head. "Maybe in the future."

Chapter Twenty-Three

There were not many in the briefing room. Cyril dropped the file on the table. Owen held the heavily stained mug in front of him with two hands as if he were about to choke the life out of it.

Liz spoke first. "It was bizarre seeing Pamela as Samuel, up close and personal, rather unnerving to be honest. She or on this occasion, he, was open, straight and without embarrassment. He admitted to having sexual relations with Smyth senior and Jenkins, the guy for whom he worked because they were kind to him. He can't be involved as he was serving on the night Tony disappeared... same goes for Jenkins so does that put them both out of the frame?"

Cyril looked at Owen who still focused on his mug. "No, if they were so friendly one could have covered for the other. Which other van was positioned close to that of Jenkins on the night Tony disappeared?"

Owen did not react but contributed to the meeting. "I can still smell the house. It was a Mrs Sonja James. Remember the first words she spoke to me and I quote, *We're buying nowt from the door so ya can bugger off."* Owen pulled a face and lifted his head. "Remember the second thing too." He turned to look at Liz. "Shit!"

"What have you remembered?" Cyril snapped.

"First thing she said when she opened the door. Do you recall, Liz?"

She pulled a thinker's expression before putting her hand to her face. She looked at Owen.

"Jesus, what's..." he didn't finish the sentence alone, Liz joined in, "*he done now?* Shit!"

"Who's he?" Cyril asked eagerly.

"Missed it, sir. We were too interested in her friends and we were eager to leave before we stuck permanently to the bloody carpet. We don't know."

Cyril bubbled inside. Was this the obvious clue that had been staring them in the face?

"Find out immediately who lives in the house and run checks on all of them. I've arranged to meet Dr Smyth tomorrow afternoon, it's been cleared with Greater Manchester Police. I want you to visit Jenkins and ask him specifically about Pamela and what his relationship is with Smyth. Anything on the missing child?"

Owen shook his head. "Seven days, sir, since the jar, so far nothing."

***

The walk home always provided Cyril with the opportunity to clear his head of any professional confusion and he certainly needed that; even the light late September drizzle brought some relief. He mulled over his conversation with Owen and Liz and could not comprehend how two professionals had missed something so crucial; a basic error that he knew had cost valuable time. He feared that it might have much more impact and that was down to him.

Crossing West Park he turned right into *The Coach*, a favourite local just round the corner from home. He watched as the glass filled with *Saltaire Pride*. He made no small talk, he was not in the mood. The barman read his expression perfectly and remained silent. To Cyril it was a sign of a good pub. Shaking his watch, he checked it against the clock behind the bar, then made a hasty retreat to a quiet alcove. He was like a cornered animal licking its wounds. The case tumbled through his mind chronologically. He thought of his boss's words, '*Tread carefully, you're only support. No bull, no broken china'.* The way he was performing, he had not even found any pots to break! How unlucky he now felt to be in full control, in the firing line. He had a review with his Chief Constable on the 26th but had little concrete evidence to present, only strong possibilities. Everyone believed according to the way the evidence had been located, that it had been left deliberately, the person committing the crimes was crying out to be caught. Cyril drank the remains of his pint. So why had he not caught them? He scanned a local paper that had been left on a table opposite and noticed the heading, *Harrogate Police*... He decided to steal his gaze away without reading on, he felt bad enough as it was.

***

Owen noted that the van was in the same spot on the driveway as when he and Liz had called on their first visit. He observed too that the tyres were rather flat. Looking around he also noticed that rust marks from the chassis had discoloured the flagged driveway, the vehicle had not moved for some time.

As on the previous occasion Mrs Jenkins came to the door.

"DS Owen, we've met before. I came to interview your husband about the missing youth at The Stray Fair. Is Mr Jenkins home?"

She smiled warmly. "Sorry, he's not. He's at one of those conventions in Birmingham, catering equipment and the like. I think he's after changing his trailer for something more modern but he never tells me anything. Work and sleep, work and sleep, that's all he ever does."

"Doesn't he use this one?"

"Not for over a year, just sits there blocking the light and spoiling the view! He messes about inside it often enough."

"Can I look inside?"

"I don't have a key, he won't let me in, it's the same with the garage where he keeps his fridges and stores. In reality I've enough to do with the house so what he gets up to in there is his business. He's very particular you know. Would you like a cup of tea?"

"Thank you, Mrs Jenkins, I would, it's been a long day."

"So where does he keep the van he uses now?"

"It's one of those trailers, they're more convenient. He stores it in the car park of *The Royal Oak*, pays for it mind. When Bruce is working his street licence permits his use of a parking area on the A59, that's when he's not doing shows and fairs."

Owen went into the lounge, the room was tidy and well organised. Mrs Jenkins could be heard in the kitchen. Owen took a moment to look at the questions he had prepared.

"I believe from Pamela Shepherd that your husband is fastidious in matters of hygiene."

There was a pause and then she came into the lounge carrying a tray.

"I've brought some cake, too. Can't have tea without cake, not in Yorkshire anyhow. Now what did you ask me?"

"Hygiene, Mrs Jenkins."

"Yes, I'm sure that he's suffered from Obsessive Compulsive Disorder, ever since I've known him. He's not in the Howard Hughes league, doesn't walk on tissues, but he's pretty bad. I even sprayed my hands after washing them with this new stuff he brought home before I cut the cake, so you'll not catch anything in this house. Sad thing is, I'm getting as bad as him. Beware officer, if you live with someone long enough you turn into them." For some reason Owen immediately thought of Cyril and felt a shiver run up his spine. "What do you need to see him about? Can I help at all?"

"Can I see the stuff you put on your hands, please?"

She stood and moved into the kitchen, returning with a black, hand-pump spray bottle. "There's no label, that's how it comes."

Owen sprayed some on his hands before rubbing them together. "I can eat this lovely cake now," he said and smiled. "I couldn't keep this could I? My mum said that cheek would get me anywhere."

"No trouble, he's got enough to sink a ship."

Owen ate the cake, passing on a number of compliments. Had Cyril been there he would have squirmed at his obsequiousness but the lady of the house absorbed his words of praise as if they were rare in her world.

"What do you know about Pamela Shepherd?"

"Lovely lady, clean and always on time. She's helped Bruce quite a lot since I did my back in. He couldn't manage without her to be honest with you."

"Has he ever talked about her past, what she did before she helped Bruce?"

"Doesn't tend to talk about work much but he has told me that she's had it rough and that some people have treated her very badly in the past but he hasn't gone into any detail. Nothing to do with me, I suppose. More tea?"

"Does he have anyone else help out if Pamela is busy?"

"Occasionally. He's mentioned a Samuel but I've never met him. Strangely, he lives in Hampsthwaite too."

"When are you expecting him home, Mrs Jenkins?" Owen licked his finger and dabbed up the crumbs from his plate.

"Should be back Thursday, hopefully not having spent a small fortune. To be honest, he makes a good living and as he says, he needs to keep ahead of the opposition."

Owen thought of Sonja James. "Not if Sonja James is the competition he doesn't."

"So, you've met the lovely Sonja have you officer? She's had the sharp edge of my tongue on many occasion, I'll tell you. Filthy woman and her boyfriend is no better."

Owen slipped into his innocent mode. "Who's he then? I've met her and for your information only, I've stuck to her hall carpet, but unfortunately he wasn't home. Is he the only other person in the house?"

"Bloody herd of them, excuse my French. All her kids by different men, trollop! Thought you'd be familiar with 'em all. Tried to trap Bruce she did, silly man, he nearly fell for her mischievous charms... all short skirt and sex that's her. Can't keep sex out of the bedroom!"

Owen breathed in. When she was in full sail Mrs Jenkins certainly grew in stature. She reminded him of a robin, small but as bold as brass.

"So who's the boyfriend now?"

"Someone not from the housing estate, a farmer, I heard. She'll likely tell you he doesn't live there to protect whatever benefits she probably claims."

"Mrs Jenkins, you've been a great help. Thanks for this." He held up the hand spray. "The cake was wonderful."

Owen stood and moved towards the door.

"Officer, one more thing. I don't know how to say this but since my back injury I've not been, let's put it sensitively, dutiful as a wife and I know that Pamela and Bruce enjoy each other's company occasionally. That's all right by me, in fact it takes away a degree of pressure, so you see, there's nothing for him to hide. Feel better for telling someone that. Thank you."

She opened the door and Owen left. Within three minutes she removed a mobile phone from a cupboard and dialled, by which time her demeanour had changed considerably. After the call, she removed the SIM card from the phone before moving into the kitchen.

***

Liz was still sitting at the computer when she really should have been home. There was no record of a male living at the address for Sonja James, only Sonja and four kids, all girls varying in age from six to sixteen. The local Neighbourhood Support Team had visited on more occasions than was healthy and Social Services had been involved with parenting skill issues identified by the schools. A dysfunctional family if ever there was one. Checking the file she finally discovered the name of a male who had been in the house on one of the visits. She blinked as she read it. Jason Gregson. "Like bees to bloody honey," she said out loud.

Chapter Twenty-Four

Cyril stood looking at the jar containing the anatomical specimen. He tilted his head to one side and spread his fingers to ascertain the object's length.

"Feeling inadequate, Cyril?" Julie asked with a giggle.

Cyril blushed. "Are you sure it's from a human being?"

"One day I'll explain why it looks longer that it should, but not today and only when I know your male ego is not so vulnerable! Good of Owen to drop this in late last night, your Forensics' bill is growing longer than our friend there." She turned to look at the jar and laughed. "I also don't relish getting into work at..." she checked her watch... "seven in the morning. Forensics have done the tests on the Hypochlorous Acid found on the boy's body and compared it to the product here which we presume is the patented cleanser produced by Dr Smyth. They are identical. You might like to have someone look at his client list but I also suggest you take a look at his friends and those working on its production. It goes without saying that when something is new to the market, samples are often distributed and believe me, you wouldn't need much of this to do a thorough cleanse of a corpse."

"I'm seeing him this afternoon. Have you got the notes on the test results for the good Dr Smyth to see?"

Julie slid the file across the table.

He left to make one more call before Peter Lee, the boy who drank from the bottle alongside Carl Granger, set off for school.

***

The black, hand-pump bottle sat in front of Cyril. "It's the same as that used to clean Tony Thompson's body." He paused. "I called on Peter Lee this morning, the lad who drank from the bottle discovered at Stray Rein. He did a double take and said that the bottle was identical to the one they drank from apart from its not having the pump-action top. Is that a coincidence, or is it a mass marketed bottle? We're checking."

Liz tapped the white board. "You were right about Gregson's son, he's Sonja James's ex-boyfriend. Like you, sir, I had an early start. Stuart Park and I, well, we paid her a visit and believe me she doesn't make good viewing in a morning. Gregson doesn't visit any longer. The Internet has obviously had an effect... the eldest daughter's expecting his child. She's sixteen, just! Sonja also believed he was grooming the next one too when he was looking after them. Can I bring him in?"

"What's her name?"

Liz checked her notes. "Kylie James."

"And the name of the girl with the two lads in Gregson's cold store?"

"Certainly not Kylie."

"Get a DNA sample and see if she's been in the store. I'll organise a warrant. Get the Response Team and bring in Jason Gregson and seize any computer equipment in the house. Owen what do you know?"

"Mrs Jenkins makes a brilliant cake." He looked at Cyril and Liz who were rather taken aback. "Also, doesn't mind her husband having sex with a bloke, not that she knows he's a male. She likes Pamela and owing to her difficult circumstances turns a blind eye, but we knew that. What you didn't know was that Samuel also helped Bruce out when Pamela was unavailable, so how does that work? We also have an old van on the drive and a locked garage, plus his catering trailer is stored in *The Royal Oak's* car park. I've checked and it's there at the moment. There's a CCTV camera belonging to the pub that looks onto the car park so I doubt that any illegal activity takes place there. I've also checked with NEC and a large catering exhibition and show is on for the next three days. According to their records Jenkins has a trade pass for three..." Owen did not finish.

Stuart Park burst in holding his iPad. “Face time image, sir. Sent in by a local Community bobby who was called to Bachelor Gardens. They found this at the end of the road.”

Cyril looked at the images. The plastic bag clearly held the corpse of what he assumed to be Carl Granger but also what appeared to be a second child.

“It’s Alan Clegg and he’s alive, bound, gagged and bagged but alive. There’s also another jar of honey. Paramedics are on their way as are Forensics. We’ll be getting Alan away before the SOCOs do their stuff.”

“On the eighth day he delivered the clothing.” Cyril said without any triumph in his voice. “We’ve spooked someone into action. All we need to find out is who.”

***

The whole of Bachelor Gardens, a narrow lane and a cul-de-sac, were sealed off and further tape and officers were positioned just after the cut through for Burns Way. Tape fluttered in the light breeze. Owen parked on Burns Way and walked through the pedestrian cutting, showing his ID to the two PCSOs who were keeping a gathering group of spectators and journalists at a designated distance. He could smell the treatment works.

Walking down the lane, Owen glanced at the allotments to his left and the irony did not escape him. This person really knew how to stage a show, what with gardens and the treatment works, he had a double hit.

The lane alongside the car park was full of vehicles. Further lengths of blue and white tape stretched across the gravel entrance and another PCSO secured the perimeter. The blue flashing lights of the paramedic response vehicle cast their ethereal light onto the browning leaves that overhung the footpath running to the right. Owen stared at the bagged body, now leaning slightly to one side. It was as if someone had been delivered of premature twins, one still trapped within the amniotic sac whilst the other child was out in the open. That one,

Alan, lay on a foil blanket, an oxygen mask attached to his face. A police constable held a saline bag as the paramedic secured the line into Alan's right wrist. Nobody else entered the area in order to protect any Forensic integrity. Within five minutes Alan was transferred to the waiting ambulance before it moved slowly away from the scene. Within minutes the siren's wail could be heard.

The Forensic team moved in. Owen felt a hand on his shoulder.

"Dr Pritchett."

"Left you to it has he, David?"

"Owen, ma'am. He's on a house call. He predicted this, the date I mean when the body would be found, but he didn't think we'd have Siamese twins. Which sad bastard puts a live kid in the same bag as a dead one?"

"He had to in order to double bag them. He's lucky he was found in time otherwise you'd have had two dead ones."

Julie moved to the rear of her car and changed. "You know Hannah?"

"Cyril mentioned her from the last crime scene. Her photographs were good."

Julie could see that Owen was not really paying her any attention he was too engrossed looking at the body.

"Dr Pritchett, there's another jar by the body, I believe. As soon as you can I want to see pictures of it and if you can manage, the contents, that is if Hannah can." He smiled at Julie knowing full well that she'd have the pictures to him forthwith.

Standing by the fence, Owen's eyes scanned the field oblivious to the activities of the Forensic Team behind him. He could no longer smell the aroma from the water treatment works at the end of the lane. He smiled inwardly, Sewage Works he knew them as, and that was if he was being polite, now water treatment, funny how the Water Board gilded the lily.

Hannah came over to Owen. She held the camera so that he could see the shots she had taken. He made notes.

Poena Honey - Handwritten in black ink – Looks to be the same style of writing as previous jars - Nothing on the inside of the label - Contains object.

He looked up at Hannah.

“Dr Pritchett suggests it’s a tongue as before. We believe it says, *Lies kill.* We’ll know more when we have it back at the lab.”

Owen made further notes and then thanked her as he was turning away.

“Hannah, I don’t know what time I’ll finish tonight but would you fancy a drink?”

She smiled. “Sorry, no thanks.” She ducked back under the tape.

Owen turned and walked up the lane. The smell returned accompanied by an even stronger taste of rejection, the combination of which seemed to make him feel nauseous.

***

Cyril pulled into the car park of the small industrial unit. The M62 had been particularly slow. He often felt thankful he lived where he did, he had had his fill of inner-city policing. The memories were often nightmares, he did not care to dwell on the past. He stared at the sign above the door of the unit, Munditia Chemicals Ltd.

Dr Smyth came into the small reception area after Cyril had rung the bell.

“Detective Chief Inspector Bennett I presume?” He held out his hand.

Smyth was taller than he had imagined and extremely handsome. His hair was obviously treated with chemicals but had a subtle greying to the temples.

“How may I help you?”

They soon settled into what looked like a staff room and meeting room. A large table sat in the middle surrounded by eight chairs. The walls were filled with charts apart from one board that contained photographs of smiling families in what looked to be Africa.

"The reason we're here, sir, the only reason! If we can bring cheap, hygienic, safe drinking water to increasing numbers of people at no cost then we have succeeded. The product here will do that but it will also sell in Europe and hopefully worldwide, bringing an additional revenue stream. All the profits will go where the people need them most. Sorry! I bang my drum sometimes too loudly."

"Creditable in this century of greed." Cyril was sincere. "Dr Smyth, when did you first meet Pamela Shepherd?"

"My bête noire, Chief Inspector? Straight to my solar plexus, no foreplay I see. Well, I met Pamela in about 1999 to 2000 in Manchester. I was on business and came across her in a bar. One thing led to another and there we have it."

"You knew she was transgender at that time?"

"Yes, beautiful as she was, let's say I had an inkling. The venue gave a clue." He smiled. "And yes, I'd been attracted to what some people refer to as lady-boys for a while. Before you ask, I was married with kids, happily I thought, but I was attracted to them. I worked hard and played hard in those distant days."

"When were you first aware that you were seeing your child's teacher?" Cyril had neither the time nor the patience to dance around Smyth's sensibilities. Besides were not all scientists supposed to be calculating and clinical?

"Funnily enough it was a while. Things slip out, no pun intended, Inspector. I believe it was when I overheard a telephone conversation, I just put two and two together."

"The surname wasn't the clue?"

"What Shepherd?"

"Dixon."

"Samuel Dixon was my son's teacher, Pamela was known to me as Shepherd. Anyway, I'm sure you know all of this or you wouldn't be here. My son overheard my wife and me arguing and then rumours spread at school. Adrian said that he had recognised Pamela when he was in Manchester, which was his initial lie. Firstly, he experienced the back of my hand, closely followed by the trauma of an unstable home life as his parents' relationship self-destructed. It wasn't pretty I can assure you. He believed the false accusations of sexual impropriety which of course, the school had to take seriously. If the police had been involved, my sexual propensity would have made the press, which in turn would have killed my business. There was only one sensible course of action. Fortunately, the school had its reputation to protect so, Chief Inspector, it became a game of damage limitation and the only one to lose out was Samuel. Technically, Samuel Dixon did not exist, neither Pamela his alleged girlfriend nor the school wished to be associated with the man."

Cyril sat back and let the last statement sink in.

"What's your relationship like with your son?"

"He followed my lead professionally but that's as far as it goes. He's benefitted from my largesse, nothing was rejected only a personal father-son relationship. I made my bed, Inspector."

"When did you last see him?"

"We occasionally see each other at professional conferences but other than that, never."

"His mother?"

"The same. She receives her monthly cheque and is happy."

"What about Bruce Jenkins?"

"I met Bruce a year ago when I was demonstrating this new product at a catering show. I try to cover all bases, medical, care homes and catering; they are all potentially huge markets. Anyway, I wanted a few companies to trial the product so they were offered it at a discounted price. He accepted and the feedback has been very positive."

"Did you deliver the product?"

Smyth shook his head. "Went by courier."

"If I were to use your product at a crime scene, would it remove all traces of DNA?"

"DNA is organic. Simple answer or scientific bullshit?"

"Simple. I'm a copper."

"Without doubt and without trace."

Cyril slipped the file Julie had given him across the table. Smyth looked through it.

"They could have done the same with fire, bleach, acid and many other ways and products."

Cyril collected the file. "Thank you for answering my rather frank questions. I hope that you'll co-operate and be patient with us. I'd like a list of all your customers to date, the names of people who work here and details of the producers of the product."

"That's easy as far as the last two are concerned. There are five employees working here either full or part-time as we make the product here from components bought in. I'll need ten minutes to copy a list of my clients."

"One last question, why *Munditia*?" Cyril pointed to the logo.

"Latin for Hygienic. Sums up the product perfectly." He smiled, leaving to copy the list.

On his return he handed it to Cyril and shook his hand. He had also brought in a cardboard box. "Please, a gift." He offered Cyril the box containing twelve plastic hand sprays.

"Sorry, don't be offended but I can't." Cyril smiled. "But the offer is appreciated."

Having been in Smyth's company for about an hour, Cyril felt sure that he was neither a kidnapper nor a murderer. He had nothing to hide. He glanced at the file on the passenger seat as the traffic crawled towards the M606. He decided to head home via Bradford.

Chapter Twenty-Five

Jason Gregson sat in the same interview room he had previously occupied. He stared at the walls. Cameras eyed him from two corners. He could feel the sweat under his arms, a mild smell of ammonia drifted to his nostrils, transferred by his increasing body heat. He had grown more confused from the moment they cautioned him. To his left sat his lawyer. Liz entered the room.

"Mr Gregson, may I remind you that this interview is being recorded and that you are under caution. Do you understand the legal implications of that?"

He looked at his lawyer who nodded to him.

"Yes."

"At the moment we have seized two computers and a phone from your property. Do you have other pieces of technology or the use of other computers capable of Internet access?"

"No."

"Your machines are being assessed by our technical Forensic team under strict guidelines. Now, please tell me about your involvement with Sonja James."

"I met Sonja just because she sold burgers from her van. When I was working I'd often see her van in the layby and would get a coffee or burger. One thing led to another."

"What the coffee led to the burger or a burger led to the coffee?" Liz played a cruel game, sensing his embarrassment.

"No! No! To..." he paused momentarily. "To sex, like."

"We're all adults here, Mr Gregson. How long have you known her, let's say, intimately?"

"Just over a year. I couldn't stay there at her place what with the kids and as you'll know, she couldn't come to mine for obvious reasons but we managed."

"Did you use the cold store for these liaisons?"

Jason nodded and then looked at his lawyer.

"You have to answer the question."

"Yes, sorry but that's not against the law."

"Did you take anyone else there?"

There was a long pause. "Yes."

"Who?"

"I took..." He again glanced at his lawyer who nodded. "I took Kylie, Sonja's daughter."

"When was this?"

"August, she was sixteen in July."

"Convenient that, Jason. Were you eagerly waiting for her to turn sixteen, were you, gagging for it, I think the modern term is?"

Jason lowered his head. "Yes, I waited and no I wasn't. I knew that it would be wrong otherwise. She did all the pushing. She'd had sex before, loads of times she told me but not with me."

"Did Sonja know?"

"Did she know? She encouraged it. She was seeing someone else. Christ, I don't know how she had time to serve food when she was parked in that layby, regular customers were always popping in. Sorry I didn't mean..."

Liz waved her hand.

"I'd drive by and there'd be a wagon in the layby and the food van would be closed up. On my way back the wagon would be gone and she'd be open. She didn't only make money from burgers."

"Did you pay Sonja, Mr Jenkins?"

"No."

"Did you pay Kylie?"

"No."

"Did you ever take pictures of Kylie for personal or public use?"

"No."

"Was it Kylie who used the cold store with the two boys. Did you watch? Take pictures? Is that why Forensics found evidence of a camera attachment so that you could watch back home?"

"No, no, I wouldn't do that. What are you saying?"

"We know it was used, don't we? Be convenient that... you spying, watching the fumbling youths with the experienced Kylie. Make good video footage that."

"No, I didn't and as far as I know it wasn't her but she might have told others about the place and so they broke in and used it."

"Have you touched Kylie's younger sister, Mr Gregson?"

Jason frowned and moved back in his chair. "Certainly not. She's thirteen for goodness sake. What the bloody hell do you think I am?"

"We're in the process of trying to establish that, to find out just what you are, Mr Gregson and only evidence and time will reveal that to the court. What we do know is that a man of forty-three likes having sex with young girls of sixteen. Do you think that's acceptable? You then stopped seeing her when you heard that she's pregnant."

"One girl, one experienced, willing girl and no I did not stop seeing her when I was told she was pregnant. I would accept the responsibility."

There was a long pause.

"Have you considered that it might not be my client's child?" his lawyer added, looking directly at Liz.

"I could count on this hand the number of times we did it and I know as I keep telling you, she had others lots of others."

Liz looked at the lawyer and raised an eyebrow as high as she could. "We can hold you here for twenty-four hours but we should have the results from you hard drives sooner."

For the second time the lawyer spoke. "I should like to request a prenatal paternity test be carried out once the results of the computer analysis have been presented, should the evidence prove in my client's favour. He is innocent and may not be responsible for the pregnancy. If the computers are clear then he has broken no law, he has merely had sex with a consenting adult."

Liz frowned but knew there was nothing further she could do. "We'll await the computer analysis and look to cross other bridges then. I'm recommending to the CPS that conditional bail be set so that that you can leave the station. Your lawyer and the Custody Sergeant will explain the conditions to you." She reluctantly smiled before leaving the room.

She knew from her experience that Jason was likely to be telling the truth. His answers were direct and swift. She believed strongly that someone was setting him up. She doubted the child was his but considered that, for Sonja James, the son of a wealthy farmer made a good catch for her wayward daughter, a catch that was proving not to be the sharpest knife in the box. Bail was essential as going back to his father was more of a deterrent than Jason sitting in a cell at the station.

***

Cyril paced the Command Room as ANPR results (Automated Number Plate Recognition) were being checked for the whereabouts of Bruce Jenkins's car. He had also contacted telecommunications for details of all calls made to and from Jenkins's home. He knew that if there were any incriminating calls being made regarding the case, then unregistered mobiles would be used, but you just never knew, these minor details still had to be checked.

"Confirmation that his vehicle was logged at one of the ANPR cameras situated at the NEC before the bodies could have been dumped, sir."

Cyril knew that with cloned plates anything was now possible and with over one and a half million cars on the road using them, it was not a rare phenomenon. All he could do was interpret the evidence with which he was presented.

Cyril looked at the notes Owen had made at the crime scene. He read, *Poena Honey.* Underneath Owen had scribbled, *Goddess of Punishment, also Latin for pain, punishment, or penalty.* Cyril read it again. He was impressed with Owen's increasing linguistic talents. He had always hated Latin, even at school. He was beginning to loathe it the longer this case continued.

He checked his watch and shook it but failed to check it again. He had endured enough of this day.

"What news from the hospital?" he asked a uniformed DC whilst leaning on the table at which she was sitting. The officer checked the computer screen.

"According to the last report, Alan is doing just fine, we have an officer there full-time as procedure." She smiled. "Well done, sir, one safely returned, it could have been worse."

And did he know it. Moving away he dug into his pocket for his phone and rang Julie but it went straight to the answerphone. "Julie, on my way home. Call me if company would be welcome. Thanks."

Cyril avoided *The Coach*; he knew that if he went in, he would only stagger out. Turning into the snicket that led to Robert Street his phone rang. It was Julie.

"Romeo, Romeo. Most men send their ladies roses and chocolates, you, Cyril Bennett, send me plastic wrapped corpses but this time one was left alive. I can assume from finding a live one, my Sherlock Holmes has a criminal on the run? Come over, I'll rustle up something."

"Wonderful lady. I'll be fifty minutes I need a shower and to collect my pipe and fiddle. Is that alright?"

"Wine's already breathing." She hung up and Cyril felt suddenly more energised than he had done in the last few hours.

***

Cyril watched Julie sip from the large glass. Her hair was what he called scrunched along the top of her head. Small curls hung haphazardly by her temples. The style suited her.

"You look stunning. The meal was wonderful and the wine is perfect. Were they oven chips?"

Julie put her glass down and dropped her head into her hands.

"Yorkshire Men!" she whispered. "What became of the fine art of romantic conversation? Were they bloody oven chips?" She spread a fake smile across her face and shook her head. "Cheers, Romeo. Of course they were oven chips."

"What have I said now?"

Julie left the table and moved to the sofa before settling down. She went through her findings, they were as expected. The honey tested the same as that in the other jars, handwriting matched, as did the enclosed tongue section removed post mortem. As in the last case it was tattooed but this time with the words *Lies kill.* Again the body had been cleaned with the same chemical and double bagged initially, but left in only one. To date no incriminating evidence was found and again a pen drive was carefully lodged in the oesophagus. It had been couriered to the Jeffrey's Lab in the late afternoon. She also mentioned that Forensics had managed to examine Alan for evidence but it would be unlikely that anything would be found considering the multiple cross-contamination from paramedics.

Cyril raised his glass. "No more work," he protested. His brain was a thick fog. He closed his eyes.

"Cyril Bennett, you'd better have some energy after all those..." she paused, "oven chips or you'll find another specimen jar in my office... I could label them little and large!" She went towards the bedroom hiding a grin.

Cyril drained the remaining wine suddenly feeling recharged.

Chapter Twenty-Six

Brenda Jenkins requested a table for two in a quieter part of the café. The waitress recognised her as a regular and asked how she was.

"I have this one, is it acceptable?"

She smiled knowing it was perfect, it was Brenda's regular table.

With more than a little relief, she deposited the cardboard box she carried on the floor before sliding it against the wall with her foot. She looked at the marks that had formed on her hand, the weight of the box had been a struggle. She sat and perused the menu, why she knew not as her order was always the same. She chatted briefly as her order was taken before beginning to rub her sore, ridged hand. The waitress brought her order. Brenda stared at the Fat Rascal that was delivered on a small plate, cleverly giving the impression that the scone like cake was larger than it actually was. The café was busy, even for a Tuesday. She sipped her tea. A Fat Rascal and tea had always been a favourite of hers. She picked a plump raisin from the side of the large scone and popped it into her mouth. At the same moment a man's hand gripped her shoulder.

"Forbidden fruit, Brenda? You can't get away with anything these days."

She was neither surprised nor amused. She pointed to the empty chair in front of her and, as if disciplining a naughty child, demanded he sit down. She looked him in the eye. There was no warmth, no welcome.

"You're late."

***

The official police interview with Lisa Smyth, Brewster's estranged wife, confirmed that she had discovered his fetish for transsexuals early on in their marriage. Although she had tried to work things out it had proved impossible, particularly when she noticed that some of her own clothing was beginning to disappear, especially her expensive lingerie. She also had no doubt that he was wearing it for work. When the marriage failed, she no longer communicated with Brewster, the house became hers and money was transferred into her account every month. She was happy with that. It also established that she still saw Adrian but not as often as she would have hoped, as his profession demanded a great deal of his time. He travelled widely, both on the continent and within the U.K. What she was unhappy about was made very clear. She believed her son had been badly treated by the school and by his father. This incident of a sexual nature involving his teacher had not only been hurriedly dealt with, in her opinion, but the true facts had never really emerged. She was convinced that he had been made the scapegoat, thereby saving his father's reputation and that of the school. Cyril closed the file. He checked his diary and noted that an appointment had been made for Wednesday afternoon with Dr Adrian Smyth who would be attending a conference in Leeds on that day.

***

Brenda Jenkins left the café and trundled down Montpelier Parade, glancing occasionally in the various shop windows whilst contemplating the finer points of the recent conversation that had lasted the best part of an hour. It was such a relief not to have to carry the box. She would slowly trace her path back up the hill, cross by the Cenotaph and walk the short distance down Cambridge Road. Once at the bus station she would wait for her 2B bus to take her home. Her final destination would be Fieldway, a short walk to her bungalow.

***

The cardboard box now occupied Brenda's seat. He leaned across the table and attached a self-adhesive address label before paying the bill. Smiling, he waved to the waitress as he left the café. He too crossed by the Cenotaph before turning left heading for Oxford Street. Once there he would call into the DHL Service Point and deposit the box for delivery. Apart from the bill at the café, he had done well out of the deal. He had one more task and then it would be time for home.

***

Cyril stared at the computer screen as the Forensic analysis report on the tests carried out on Alan Clegg were uplifted. Owen and Liz stood by each shoulder. To the casual observer they resembled the Holy Trinity, but considering the way the case was developing, others might say they resembled the three wise monkeys.

"Positive DNA Forensic match for Bruce Jenkins, a short hair with follicle. Thought you mentioned in the report he was fat and bald with funny toenails?"

"Hair round the back and a bit of a comb-over but we're talking thin." Owen demonstrated with his hand. "Think more Friar Tuck than Yul Brynner."

"Thank goodness for that at least, it's a first! It appears to have been trapped inside the bag, attached to the tape that was used to close it at the top. Adhesive must have formed a hermetic seal protecting the hair from the sanitized spray of the cleanser. There's absolutely nothing else to go on."

Owen looked puzzled. "We know that he's been away in Birmingham so how the hell can he be in two places at once unless someone else dropped the bag?"

"What's the time difference between his car being picked up on ANPR cameras and the discovery of the body?"

"We checked, sir, after I visited Mrs Jenkins if you recall. He was at the NEC before the bag was dropped."

"His car was Owen, his car was. It only tells us that his car number plate was registered at that time. Ring his wife and see where he's staying and get the local force to pay him a visit. All the usual stuff, photo ID, prints to them etc. If it's possible, see if they can put a call out at the Exhibition Centre. All we can do now is wait. What news on Alan?"

Liz smiled. "He's home and seems no worse for the experience. Amazing how resilient kids are."

"What about Gregson, Liz?"

"His computers were clean apart from what we already knew. It appears that he was telling the truth. We had another word with Sonja James and she reluctantly confirmed that Kylie had been sexually active before Gregson was involved and with multiple partners. Her excuse was that she was mature for her age! We've applied to get a court order for the prenatal paternity test as there's reluctance on Sonja's part. Looks like mother's little game of finding a wealthy man, no doubt either to fleece or possibly to blackmail, could well be up. Social Services are now taking an active interest so some good may come of it for the younger kids at least."

"In some ways I feel sorry for Jason Gregson. His life at the moment is lived between a rock and a hard place. I personally don't understand why he doesn't just go."

"No answer at the Jenkin's house. Do you want me to call?"

"Try again if we get nothing from the NEC. If there's still nothing, go round."

Chapter Twenty-Seven

Brenda Jenkins turned the key in the front door, pushed it open and breathed a sigh of relief. It had been more stressful than she had anticipated, what with depositing the bodies earlier and then the box. So much for her bad back. If she did not have one before she should have by now. She put her handbag and the keys on the side table and looked in the hall mirror. Her eyes shone, she had no regrets. It was true what had always been said about revenge, that it was sweet and best served cold. She had delivered both. He would not treat her like dirt anymore that was for sure. Licking her finger she straightened her left eyebrow before walking towards the kitchen, besides she had just spent an hour with the man who gave her more pleasure than Bruce ever could. She thought of the night before, visualising his firm body and shivered. "Don't be silly," she whispered to herself. "You need a cup of tea, Brenda, and maybe a cold shower, that's what you need my girl," she said out loud. It would be the pick-me-up she desperately craved. "And then you can put your feet up." She chuckled as she took the kettle to the sink.

The sound of the water filling the kettle masked the sound of any movement, but the arm that swiftly wrapped around her throat and squeezed took her completely by surprise. A slight whimper erupted briefly from her lips, but the power within the arm blocked any further protest. Her hand instinctively released the kettle in a desperate attempt to escape and clear her airway. The kettle clattered into the metal sink. Her senses suddenly became heightened and she recognised the faint smell of cologne. Her mind filled with confusion and betrayal. She could neither shout nor speak. Slowly her peripheral vision diminished, grey opacity began filling her eyes until a blurred light was the only visual acuity that remained. An animal grunt tried to form a name but failed; it was hidden, almost drowned out by the running water. The gurgling breath was just audible until there was nothing. Brenda's body went limp, her left leg kicked spasmodically twice as if she were in some macabre dance; her arms fell away. Snot dribbled slowly down towards her upper lip. It took just one further squeeze before the job was finally done.

The gloved hand unfurled from her neck and leaned over turning off the tap. The room fell silent apart from the ticking of a clock. The kettle was collected and returned to its stand, water pooling around the base. Brenda was lowered carefully to the floor. Within minutes she would be placed in one of the chest freezers that lined either side of the garage and there she would wait. She would be able to put her feet up for slightly longer than she had anticipated.

After a careful check, the front door was opened and quietly shut and locked. The figure pulled up the hood on his jacket before turning. The key was replaced under the front tyre of the van on the drive from where it had been collected. Now it was time for home.

***

"Call out at the Exhibition Centre was fruitless, sir. They're waiting for him at his hotel. His car is in the NEC car park, an officer is waiting there too. He could have been outside taking the air, who knows, it's a bloody big place. I suppose it's the last thing you expect, hearing your name called."

Owen found himself again looking at the van on the drive for the third time. There was no answer when he knocked on the front door. He moved to the lounge window, put his hand against the glass, his head against his hand and peered in. Nothing. He moved round to the back. A net curtain prevented a clear view of the kitchen but he could see there was no one in. He took out his mobile and dialled the house phone. He heard it ring. There was still no answer. He then called Cyril's mobile to give him the news. Whilst coming down, Owen had noticed a neighbour across the road standing in his front window; he was waving urgently. Owen approached him. He quickly appeared on the driveway.

"Can I help you?"

Owen removed his ID and held it out. "Looking for either Mr or Mrs Jenkins. Have you seen them today?"

"Mrs Jenkins arrived home a good couple of hours ago. She's still in as far as I know. The man who left shortly after she arrived home was alone. I had a bad feeling about that."

"Was that Mr Jenkins?"

"No, never seen him before. Went that way. Never saw him arrive for that matter, I must have been making a cuppa."

"Can you describe him, Mr...?"

"Bill, Bill McArthur. Not really, he was wearing one of them hoody things. Fairly tall and I assume not too old but I couldn't really say. I saw him pop the key back under the wheel, it's their spare. When you get older, officer, you need back up keys dotted about the place."

"So, you think she's in?"

"As far as I know."

Owen went back on the drive, located the key and opened the front door. He called but there was no reply then he noted her handbag and keys on the side. He briefly went to his car and returned before slipping on a pair of plastic overshoes and some gloves. There was nobody in the lounge. He called again. Nothing. He progressed to the kitchen. Water pooled on the floor and the work surface around the base of the kettle. He noticed one set of prints towards the back door. He moved quickly to the front door and turned down the drive to face the garage. There was a hint of a print just by the back door where there was a degree of shade and then nothing. The garage door seemed secure. He took out his mobile and dialled again.

"Secure it Owen, we're on our way. No one in and nothing out. Well done."

***

Cyril and Owen stared into the garage. A tent had been erected in front of the double open doors to prevent unwanted spectators and police tape fluttered across the bottom of the drive. A uniformed officer stood to one side. Four police vehicles were parked along what was normally a quiet road and as usual the journalists had arrived.

"She's in the left freezer. They've found a door to the rear." Owen held up an iPad. They watched as the Forensic Officer scanned the room. They could make out the bed and the commode. Cyril noted the chalk tally marks on the wall.

"They found three drums of honey, jars and labels but no tattoo equipment as yet. There were photographs of Tony and Carl on the wall facing the commode. Anything on Jenkins?"

"Nothing. According to the hotel, he wasn't seen last night and he didn't appear for breakfast. They're checking to see if he used his ticket today, it should be on their system. Has anyone thought of looking in the boot of his car? Have the CCTV images been checked for the date he arrived?"

Cyril looked at Owen and frowned. "Someone's clearing up."

"The last jar, sir, Goddess of Punishment. Where's Pamela Shepherd right now?"

Cyril called Liz. "Get over to Pamela's aunt's immediately, don't ring or forewarn her. Take protection and have backup standing by. If she's there and all looks normal call me immediately."

"Sir, call just in. A cleaner has found Jenkins's body in another room of the hotel. The room was registered to a Dr Smith. We're awaiting CCTV."

"Ilkley, Liz, as quickly as possible. Be careful!"

Cyril turned to Owen. "Pay a call on Dr Brewster Smyth." Cyril jotted down the address. "I want to know where he's been since my meeting with him. Also check to see where his car's been. This place here is going to be thoroughly stripped for evidence."

***

Liz sat in the car and checked that the West Yorkshire Police backup vehicle was in position. A light misty rain swept from west to east smudging the view of the moor well beyond the station at the top of the road. It had been wet for most of the journey. She smiled at the accompanying officer.

"Ready?"

"Ma'am." He adjusted his stab vest and his hands ran over the equipment attached to various belts, a habit of long-standing.

There were no outward signs of occupation but she knew someone was home as the aunt was housebound. Liz knocked loudly on the door.

Pamela Shepherd opened the door. Liz did not know what to expect but the look of astonishment on Pamela's face left no doubt as to the fact that she was not expected.

"Liz, this is a nice surprise. I thought it might be the carer. Are we meant to meet today?"

Liz shook her head. "May we come in?"

The familiar smell of lavender grew more strongly the further they entered.

"Is everything all right?" Pamela asked. There was no guile in her query.

"Have you been home all day?"

"Apart from shopping and a coffee whilst the carer was here, yes. I thought that was her, she left her umbrella."

"How long did it take, Pamela?"

"What, leaving the house? No more than an hour. Why?"

"I have some bad news, you'll hear it soon enough but as you know these people you need to be informed. Mr and Mrs Jenkins have both been found dead." Liz observed Pamela's body language looking for the slightest hint of guilt the exact opposite was evident.

Pamela stood as if frozen. She put out a hand to hold onto a winged, high-backed chair for support, her other hand moved towards her mouth.

"An accident?" Pamela managed to collect herself and ask.

"Forensics are investigating but from the evidence we have at the moment it looks as though they were both murdered."

Pamela's face screwed into a look of incomprehension. "Why? They were such kind people."

There was that word again. Why was everyone kind? "Sit down. What I'm about to say to you may come as a shock."

Pamela sat.

Liz looked at the officer and nodded towards the kitchen. "She needs a brew and so do I."

He moved through and Liz heard him opening cupboards and then filling the kettle.

"Don't make too much noise, my aunt will be upset. I've just managed to get her to sleep. She was awake most of the night."

"We think whoever killed them was responsible for the kidnap and murder of the two Harrogate boys. We believe that the perpetrator has been spooked and that he's now clearing up. What his connection was with the Jenkins is unknown at this stage, but obviously there was some involvement. Once checks on the property have been completed we should have a much clearer picture, but until then we can only guess."

The officer brought in two mugs of tea then stood to one side.

"Drink it!" Liz urged.

Pamela wrapped her hands around the mug and sipped. "I was involved with Bruce. Am I safe?"

Liz looked directly into Pamela's eyes. There was something in what she had just asked that brought a kick to her inside. "Should you be a target?" Liz kept direct eye contact and Pamela looked into the mug.

"I thought you might know. The last time we met you said that the missing boys might have some bizarre connection with the incident I experienced at school all those years ago. I'm sure that's not the case. Besides I'm not going to spend my life looking over my shoulder, I've enough on my plate with…" She did not finish but sipped more of the tea.

Liz looked at her colleague and raised an eyebrow. "We'll place a WPC with you for forty-eight hours, by which time we should know more."

Pamela shook her head. "You're not listening, thanks but no thanks. We'll be fine."

The officer sneezed. "Excuse me, the lavender, sorry."

"Pamela, is that Samuel I can hear? Pamela? Pamela?" The voice drifted down the stairs sounding feeble and weak.

Pamela looked at the officer. "Thanks for that."

"Are you sure about a WPC? I can't force one on you but it's my advice that you have some support, even for a few hours."

"No, thanks. Now I must attend to my aunt."

The officer stood by the car door and inhaled deeply. "It was that bloody lavender, brought tears to my eyes. Seemed worse in the kitchen."

Handing him a tissue, Liz sat in the car and called Cyril.

***

Owen had spoken with Dr Brewster Smyth and two witnesses corroborated his whereabouts for the dates in question. He had been nowhere near Birmingham and neither had his car. Strangely Smyth seemed more upset that he had lost a customer than concerned that he had been questioned.

***

"Bennett."

"Sir, it's all quite bizarre really. Instead of confronting a murderer I'm now consoling a frightened puppy. She's really very upset. We don't know if Pamela will be targeted because she knew the Jenkins or if the case revolves around her past, but she adamantly refused some short-term protection. It'll upset her aunt having strangers in the house. Either way there's a slim possibility that she might be a target but I can't force an officer on her."

"What was your gut feeling, Liz?"

"I don't know, but there's something hidden and for the life of me I can't see it."

"Did you mention that Mrs Jenkins told you that a Samuel worked for her husband when she was unavailable?"

"Deliberately kept that quiet. Do you want me to mention it?"

Cyril knew that it would be worth hanging on to that snippet as it would make no difference if Pamela already knew. It might prove valuable later.

"No, least she knows about the better at the moment. Get back here as soon as."

Chapter Twenty-Eight

Owen was sitting at his desk when Liz walked past.

"You look as though you've lost a tanner and found a farthing." Her attempt at conversation did not even warrant his eye contact. "Why was I so eager to get involved in this bloody case, Owen? Jesus, it's like riddling soot whilst turning bloody circles. I keep thinking of that song, *Girls will be boys and boys will be girls*... can't even think who sang the damned thing I'm so mentally battered."

"It's the Kinks, from their song *Lola*. My dad used to like it."

"Bloody hell, he speaks and you're right. I'm certainly mixed and muddled and it's definitely shook up."

Owen's face cracked slightly and then he pointed to the chair directly in front of him. "Have you a second? There's something I need to ask you as you're a woman, like."

Liz looked at Owen and could see that he was embarrassed. "Full of compliments, Owen, never thought you'd noticed." She observed his facial expression and realised that he was serious. "Sure, fire away, as long as it's not the birds and the bees enquiry." She smiled hoping that a joke might make him relax a little. It did not have the desired effect.

"I asked a girl out for a drink the other day and I got a flat refusal, a straight no. There was no excuse or even a maybe, just a straight no thanks. It's happened twice recently. Do you think it's because of my dress sense or do I have bad breath or body odour?"

Owen did not lift his head. He played with his hands and looked down whilst he asked the question. Liz wanted to laugh but stifled the reaction before appearing to give his enquiry serious consideration.

"You're smart enough, you don't have bad breath and you don't smell apart from on occasion when you splash some cheap aftershave all over yourself."

Owen looked up. "That was a present from Cyril last Christmas."

"Throw it and choose your own. Look, you might not be her type. Some women like big men others don't." The longer she spoke the more she felt as though she were digging a rather large hole for herself. "You're a handsome man, a catch for the right woman. Remember your job doesn't help. Look at the hours you keep, they're irregular and not ideal for a committed relationship. That's why so many coppers marry coppers, teachers marry teachers, as only they understand the dedication and time needed to do the job right. Whom did you ask out for the drink?"

"The Pathologist's new assistant, Hannah Peters."

"That's an easy puzzle to solve, Owen. She's going out with one of the Tech lads, has been for some time, so it's nothing personal. You're better off single if you ask me."

Cyril walked in. "You two, we have some results, incident room in ten. Owen, coffee please, clean cup and saucer." He smiled.

***

Owen looked at the photograph on the screen as he carried the requested coffee and placed it on the desk in front of Cyril. He was tempted to touch his forelock but then thought better of it as Cyril thanked him.

"The box you see here was delivered by courier to a Mrs Hackworth. Anyone recollect the name? If not, you've not been memorising the details of this case. Well?"

"Head teacher of the school Samuel Dixon, AKA Pamela Shepherd worked at and was dismissed from." Owen spoke with confidence after looking at something Liz had scrawled on a piece of paper and pushed towards him.

"Thank goodness at least Owen's awake."

Liz squeezed his leg and smiled.

Cyril pressed a button on the handset and another image appeared on screen. It was a collection of tattooist's equipment next to which sat a jar.

"All from the box. Honey jar, marked with the same label as the previous jar, *Poena Honey.* It appears that there is a piece of tattooed flesh within the jar and from all accounts…" He pressed the button again and a new image flashed up..." It simply says *Lying bitch.* Skin sample has been sent to Forensics for DNA testing and Lancashire Police are with Mrs Hackworth now. As you can imagine, she was somewhat shocked.

"The delivery has been traced back to Harrogate, to a Courier Service point on Oxford Road. CCTV shows a man with a goatee beard, dark glasses and a hooded jacket, the same character that was seen on tapes at the hotel where Jenkins was found, the same *kind* man with twinkly eyes as described by the kids who were given a jar in exchange for a kiss like a bee kisses a flower and finally by Sonja James, a match for the man who gave her the bottles of energy drink to distribute. This mystery man also signed the paperwork as Bruce Jenkins and gave Jenkins's address but you can see from the person's build that it's not Jenkins. Besides, Jenkins was probably dead when this box was brought in, the time, 11.46 am is marked on the copy of the receipt. We've checked CCTV for areas around Oxford Street and there was a sighting by the bus station but then nothing. Images from the camera near the Cenotaph show that he crossed carrying the box there before making the deposit. Officers are questioning shop keepers in the vicinity of that camera."

An officer walked behind Cyril and placed a note on the table. He read it.

"A waitress described seeing a regular customer with a cardboard box matching the description at about 10.30. She asked for a quiet table, a man later joined her. The waitress emphasises that the lady left without it and that the gentleman took the box out. She's identified the woman as Mrs Jenkins."

"So, we can safely assume that Mrs Jenkins knew what was in the box, therefore we can presume that the box was at the Jenkins's house and used there. So, my question is..." Cyril paused and looked at the sea of faces.

"Why move it? Why post it to the Head teacher? Why risk all of that?" Stuart Park asked.

"Why kill your partner or partners in crime?" Liz offered.

"He's done what he set out to do for whatever reason. He's tested us and so far we've failed even with the clues he's posted."

"Maybe he's now leaving a trail to some grand finale."

Cyril listened but said nothing. He sipped his tea, following the interaction within the room before asking. "Who had visible tattoos of all the people we've interviewed?"

"Jenkins, sir. On his hands and only his wife knows where else."

"Correct. The report says self-inflicted, done at home with ink and needle and not very well executed to boot. Who else?"

The room fell silent.

"Strangely, Dr Brewster Smyth had a tattoo on his arm. It wasn't really clear but I could see the shading beneath his shirt, professional and one of those popular Polynesian designs. It stood out like a sore thumb. It's funny, before that interview I would never have put scientists and tattoos in the same sentence. I'm meeting his son this afternoon. Owen, you're with me. As soon as we have anything from Forensics, both from the Jenkins's place and from the equipment from the box, I want it sending to Owen."

Chapter Twenty-Nine

The Leeds hotel reception was modern and light. Owen thumbed through the magazine that he had picked up from a rack whilst Cyril checked his nails before removing his electronic cigarette. He inhaled deeply enjoying the quiet moment. It was a blessing being able to vape inside. He watched a gentleman exit one of the lifts and approach the Reception Desk. After a few words he turned, looked across at Cyril and crossed the room.

"Detective Chief Inspector Bennett?"

Cyril stood and smiled. "Dr Smyth, thank you for making time in what I believe is a busy schedule to see us. May I introduce DS Owen?"

Smyth shook Owen's hand and then Cyril's. "No trouble, I'm away for a few weeks in a couple of days, a well-earned rest. I'm a victim of my own success and the demands on my time are crushing." He paused turned to the Receptionist and pointed towards a room to the left. She smiled and nodded. "Shall we go through to the Residents' Lounge? It will be more private."

As soon as they had sat down, coffee was brought in. "I thought you might like some refreshment, I took the trouble of ordering coffee, I hope that's all right? What can I do for you, Chief Inspector?"

Cyril briefly discussed his understanding of what had occurred at Clearmount School.

"That's a long time ago but it's an indelible memory because I was branded a liar and a trouble maker. The sexual impropriety happened. I didn't make it up." He paused as if collecting his emotions. "I discovered that my father was having a relationship with someone, an affair. My parents constantly rowed about it and this person's name came up. I knew my father secretly dressed in my mother's underwear, he didn't realise I knew at the time. I saw him when he thought I was out of the house. Anyway, Dixon, our Science teacher, was a little limp-wristed shall we say to be polite and out of the blue I mentioned inaccurately to some of the lads that I'd seen him dressed as a woman in Manchester one Saturday. "

Cyril immediately thought the branding of him as a liar was therefore correct but did not interrupt.

"It was a joke at the time, a bit of fun, a schoolboy prank but the implications proved to be devastating."

He took a drink of coffee. Owen who had been taking notes paused.

"After that some of the lads started putting items of clothing, knickers and the like, on Dixon's car and on his desk. He didn't get angry, he just sort of moved them but he always seemed to focus on me, as if he had some kind of sixth sense and knew that I was the one who had start the malicious rumour. He couldn't have known, I thought at the time, unless someone had grassed. It was only later that I realised the truth of the matter. I was held back by Dixon after a late lesson under the pretence that he wanted to go over some of the work I'd completed. He'd done this before without any worries, I guess you'd say I was the best Science student he had. On this occasion, I was standing next to his desk when he suddenly grabbed my genitals and squeezed. It came as such a shock. As he held me he told me that he knew that it was me who had started the rumour and that he would begin to make my life absolute hell. He then confided in me that he was and I remember the words clearly, *Shagging your father and I have him by the metaphorical balls too*! It was then that the abuse started, the fondling and the like. There was never penetration. It seemed to be expected more and more frequently. I was called back to his office at regular intervals. I don't even think he enjoyed it sexually, it was more a punishment, more out of revenge.

"I just couldn't take it any longer; my studies and schooling were suffering so I informed the Head, Mrs Hackworth. I couldn't mention it to my father. I also mentioned it to three mates who supported my story by fabricating their own.

We thought we'd be stronger in numbers. My father went ballistic when the Head contacted him. We boys naively thought that making a complaint in numbers would be to our advantage. How wrong we were! Little did we know that two lads would weaken. A great deal of pressure was put on me to retract the allegations. Obviously my father was looking after his own interests as well as those of his lover and the school was frightened and therefore defending its reputation and so I was sidelined."

"So, no police?"

Smyth shook his head. "Chief Inspector, I was fourteen, let down by two friends at a time when I needed them the most, but more importantly, I was discarded by my own father. The one school friend who stuck by me sadly is no more. He died in an accident, I believe."

"So what did you do about it?" Owen asked.

"When my parents separated, I never spoke to the bastard again. I was determined to be better than him. I matched his qualifications, in fact I bettered them. I gained a first in my degree and a distinction in my masters. Whenever we met, and that was only occasionally, I was usually leading the conference. It gave me a great deal of satisfaction. I would imagine him sitting there surrounded by colleagues and beneath the façade, beneath the suit and tie would be lingerie."

"And your mother?"

"She was weak too, would never stand up to him. She knew that I was being honest about the abuse but she couldn't upset my father. Amazing how your upbringing either makes you weak or makes you stronger and more determined." He drank the last of his coffee.

"Have you ever met Samuel Dixon since that time?"

Smyth shook his head. "Neither Samuel nor Pamela. Yes I'm aware of the Janus face of my abuser. It all became disgustingly clear once my father left."

"You could still seek justice irrespective of the passage of time. The police will look into the matter. Sexual impropriety with a minor carries a long custodial sentence, let alone a stigma."

"Life's too short. I've moved on. I seek neither justice nor revenge. What was in the past can now stay there."

Smyth looked at his watch. "Where does the time go? If there's nothing else?"

"I believe you're not married? Do you have a partner?"

"I'm sure as a busy policeman you know that permanent relationships and a hectic work schedule are incompatible. Are you married Chief Inspector?" He watched Cyril's shake of the head. "And you Sergeant? I rest my case, gentlemen."

Cyril stood and shook Smyth's hand. "One last thing. Your father has a large tattoo on his arm, seems rather incongruous to me that a man of science would have a tattoo of that nature."

"What my father does with his body ceased to interest me when I was fourteen, Chief Inspector, when he betrayed me. He could tattoo War and Peace over every inch of flesh for all I care. Now, if you'll please excuse me."

Dr Smyth left the room and Cyril sat down.

"Direct and to the point wouldn't you say? The good doctor used some strong language to express some vivid emotional memories, Owen. Anything from Forensics?"

Owen downloaded the waiting mail before reading the report he had received on his iPad. "DNA for both boys found at Jenkins' garage, honey matches that found in the other jars, labels, pen all match. They've recovered a mobile phone from the house but no sim card. They're conducting a more thorough search. The phone's not registered to either, it's a throw away. Forensics suggest that the house has been searched. Our killer was looking for something, probably the sim card. Both mine and Liz's DNA have been found at the scene; they're on the ball."

"What of the box?"

Owen scrolled down the page.

"It was a piece of human tongue found in the jar. The tattoo ink is identical but there's no DNA match to any of the deceased. Tattooed post mortem as with the others." Owen looked at Cyril. "Does that mean we have another body somewhere?"

Cyril put his hand to his face and rubbed his chin. "It's looking that way!"

"Give Liz a call. In the light of the latest revelation regarding Samuel Dixon, I want to pay Pamela a visit. He checked his watch. Tell her first thing tomorrow morning, and I mean first thing."

"Were you not meeting the Chief Constable, sir?"

"I have that pleasure pencilled in for this afternoon, Owen, and that will come soon enough believe me! If the meeting doesn't go too well, the way I feel right now you might make Inspector sooner than you'd hoped."

Chapter Thirty

Cyril was not a happy man after his meeting with the Chief Constable, even though his boss had appreciated the complexity of the case. The key points of the one-sided meeting tumbled in his head as he stared at the car park and breathed in fresh air. *The general public want things boxed and ticked quickly. That's your job. You wanted this, you pushed for it. They've had few answers. I know you've managed to return one child but that was more good luck than judgement. We need a man in custody, Cyril, and we want it to happen quickly so that we can all move on, particularly those unfortunate to have lost a child.*

***

"Did you know Alan Titchmarsh comes from Ilkley, sir?" Liz felt as though she had to say something. Cyril had not spoken for most of the journey, he simply blew vapour from his nostrils and looked at the view.

Cyril said nothing in reply. He looked across the fields as the mist wrapped around the lower part of the trees. After a while he broke his silence.

"It's my favourite time of the year. Such a delicate season, balanced between the heat of summer and the onset of winter. It's like the year has suddenly realised it's the beginning of the end."

"Or to be more optimistic and quote Churchill, sir, ... *the end of the beginning."*

Cyril turned to her and smiled. "Yes, you're right ... *the end of the beginning*. We've only just got into our stride."

Owen had informed her of Cyril's meeting the previous day with the Chief Constable and she realised he was now carrying the weight of the investigation heavily on his shoulders.

She took a quick glance at him. He looked tired and she had to admit it, old for his years. "Summer every time for me, sir and preferably summer along the Mediterranean."

"So how shall we find Pamela this morning, Liz? Stressed and surprised or pleased to see her new best friend?"

"She's a hard one to read that's for sure. There's something that doesn't gel. Call it female intuition but there's something."

Liz parked the car lower down the road than usual.

"A bit more of a surprise for her today, sir."

"I take it you've informed the local force of our intentions?"

Liz smiled.

There was no answer when Cyril knocked. He tried again but there was still no response.

"She'd never leave her aunt alone."

"Check next door."

Liz walked up the next path and knocked. She smiled at Cyril and waited for the door to be answered. An elderly man opened the door slightly. Liz saw the security chain. She presented her ID. "Do you know if Pamela Shepherd is in next door?"

"Not seen her today. I heard the old lady calling out but then it all went quiet, nothing strange in that though. It's a shame when they become so confused. Sometimes she thinks I'm her father when I pop round. I'm younger than her too and have known her for nearly five years now! Comes to us all." He opened the door fully. "He a copper too?"

Liz nodded, "My boss."

Liz returned. "Nothing, sir, the gentleman says he's not seen Pamela. I'm a bit concerned."

"Ring her mobile."

Liz dialled. There was no answer. Cyril opened the letterbox and heard a mobile ringing.

"Phone's inside I can hear it."

She then rang the house phone and let it ring. "Nothing, sir. Please, I'm worried."

"I'll get the local lads to force entry, life and death, Liz. No need for a warrant."

Liz held up her hand. "Just a minute." She turned back to the neighbour's house and knocked again.

"Do you know if any of the neighbours has a key?"

"A minute lass."

Liz returned with a key. "Worth a try and bingo!" She smiled at Cyril.

Both put on gloves and overshoes. On entering Cyril put his hand to his nose. "Goodness me, that's strong."

"Lavender, sir. Always smells of lavender, it's even stronger in the lounge. I'll go and check on the aunt."

Liz moved cautiously up the stairs, looking in each room she approached.

"Is that you Pamela?" the familiar feeble voice called out.

A sudden flush of relief flooded her stomach. The old girl was alive at least. She popped her head round the door. The old lady smiled. Liz realised that she thought she was Pamela.

"Is Samuel with you? I heard his voice."

"No, it's a friend, that's all. Do you need anything?"

The old lady smiled.

Liz picked up a photograph frame from the dressing table. It was clearly a picture of Pamela, her mother and aunt. The Cow and Calf rocks stood in the background. It had been taken when times were better. She then picked up another frame. This one was taken not that long ago, there was a date in the bottom left hand corner and an inscription: *To my beautiful aunt. All my love, Pamela xx.* Liz looked more carefully, taking the picture to the window. This was certainly not the Pamela she had met.

Liz went back down the stairs carrying the photograph and entered the kitchen. Cyril was looking into what was the larder. What appeared to be silicone strips seemed to be hanging from the door edges and the architrave like thick cream-coloured spaghetti.

"Sir, this is a photograph of…" She did not finish. The stench seemed to overpower the lavender, assaulting her nasal passages. She turned her head away. It was then that she noticed that Cyril was holding a handkerchief to his nose.

"That's the reason for the lavender!"

Cyril pointed inside. At the far end, bagged, in polythene in the same way as the boys' corpses sat another.

"Door was sealed with silicone making it air tight. It took some opening. The body is double bagged. It looks like the skin's smeared with honey, and a lot of it by the look of it, but it's run off parts of the face."

"What's that?"

Liz held up the photograph for Cyril to see. "This is Pamela Dixon but it's definitely not the Pamela I spoke to here, or had coffee with, absolutely not."

Cyril just pointed to the recumbent figure. His hand found the light switch. "Is that the person in the photograph?"

Liz turned slightly as the smell hit her again.

"You're not going to be sick are you, Liz?" Cyril's expression had changed. The last thing he needed was vomit.

She looked back and smiled. "I'm fine, honest."

Checking the photograph again, she then inspected the facial features as best she could considering the opacity of the polythene and the layer of honey. The face was gaunt, but even the stretched flesh trapped within the enclosed bags could not conceal the likeness. "It's the person in this photograph. We can presume it's Pamela Shepherd. She's been dead a while." Liz came back into the kitchen and looked at Cyril. "So, if that's Pamela Shepherd, who the bloody hell have I been talking to?"

Cyril did not need time to think. The interview he had held in Leeds had haunted him all night and he had been mulling it over for most of the morning's journey.

"I know the killer's name. I know who your Pamela is."

"Well, sir?"

"It's Dr Adrian Smyth, that's who you've been talking to. You've seen Smyth's image on the incident board, does he resemble the Samuel you spoke to the other day?"

"No, sir, but to be honest, I was rather taken aback when he opened the door. I was expecting Pamela."

"Call the Murder Squad in and get an arrest warrant for both Dr Adrian and Dr Brewster. I'll call for SOCO and Social Services for the lady upstairs. I'll lay you five to one that there's a DNA match with the tongue delivered to the Head teacher and the bagged corpse in the cupboard. Then I want you to pay a visit to our friendly Neighbourhood Watch bully. He might know more than he lets on. Take a photograph of that image and let's see if it rings any bells. Also get him to take you into Pamela's house. Have Owen with you, it will help convince him."

Chapter Thirty-One

Liz and Owen crunched their way down the gravel drive. Hampsthwaite was quiet for early afternoon, but as if on cue, the curtain moved slightly and Liz informed Owen that they were being watched.

Owen, deciding as usual to grasp the bull by the horns, pushed his way through the privet hedge and strode up to the door, banging his fist against the glass centre panel. Liz watched.

"Who the bloody hell..." The door swung open and Melville stood looking up at Owen who seemed to fill the space where the door should be. Owen's ID was held out directly into Melville's line of vision.

"John Melville, please step outside, now!" Owen stood to one side as Melville moved quickly onto the drive. He glanced across at Liz who could not help but smile.

"Morning, Mr Melville. Brought my own Rottweiler today. How are we apart from the usual? Please bring Pamela's key and pop round or through the hedge whichever is the more convenient."

"I can't just let you go into that house. You don't have a warrant or anything."

"If you don't co-operate with the police, I'll have to inform you that Sergeant Owen there will go into your property to search for the key. I must warn you that because of his *delicate* build he does tend to be rather clumsy. Should he fail to find the said key, we'll arrest you and take you to the station for hindering a police enquiry. Now, Mr Melville, the choice is yours."

Melville's face reddened and he blew out his lips. "What about Sam? What about the dog?"

"You'll take him for a walk whilst Sergeant Owen and I look around the property but before that I want you to tell me who this is."

Covering up the inscription Liz held up the photograph.

Melville took it. "I'll need my glasses." He went into the house returning with half-moon spectacles lodged on the end of his nose. He handed Owen the key. He also held the dog's lead.

"That I think is Pamela."

Liz was taken aback. "Are you sure?"

"Yes. Look, she lived here with her mother, I should know."

It was then that Liz tried one question that she believed might throw him.

"Did you ever meet Samuel?"

Melville laughed. "Is that a trick question, Sergeant?" He did not wait for her to reply. "Of course I met Samuel, he's a nice lad."

"Did you ever see Samuel and Pamela together, in the garden or with their mother?"

"No, only saw Samuel recently, he'd been working away. He just called to leave money for the dog. The dog seemed to know him, never any trouble."

"Did you speak to him at all?"

"It's funny that, no. He just left money and notes, usually early in the morning. A car would drop him and collect him."

"Have you kept any of the notes, Mr Melville?"

He nodded and went back into the house.

"He knows nothing, he's all wind."

Owen smiled.

Melville took the dog up the drive and Owen, followed by Liz, entered the property. It was as Liz had imagined, ordered, a little dusty but organised. Framed photographs lined the mantelpiece. She picked them up one at a time; they showed a chronological history of a disparate family. To one side was a photograph of Samuel Dixon with a class of children, the date and school name printed along the mount base. One of the boy's faces was circled and then she noticed Samuel. The same red ink had added satanic horns to his head. There were other scribbles obliterating two boys' faces which she assumed to be those of the boys who failed in their support. She then noticed the halo, only small, but carefully added above the head of one boy. The whole tragic story was there on this one photograph.

"Liz, upstairs."

Liz put the photograph down and went upstairs.

"In here."

The lock from the bedroom door lay on the carpet alongside splinters of the wooden architrave. Owen stood in the front bedroom. Writing was scrawled over the wall in thick, red felt tip pen:

Those who lie shall be made to tell the truth.
Revenge shall make the bitter become sweet.
Honey is nature's way of cleansing the body, spirit and soul.
Human kindness will reap true rewards.

Beneath the writing, a spider's web of drawn lines linked photographs and strange doodle-like drawings. Owen moved closer and studied the images. He identified Tony Thompson, but he did not recognise the name written beneath. He knew Carl Granger too but the name written below did not match the image. He then looked at the photograph of Alan. The word Alan was written beneath as if to invalidate the veracity of the other two. Further web-like lines had been drawn to connect the boys' images to an early photograph of Samuel Dixon, next to which was positioned a photograph of Pamela. To the left was a print of his father; this too had been embellished with the devil's horns and a small, satanic goatee beard. Owen tapped the beard and raised an eyebrow. Away from the web were two separate images, the first of Bruce Jenkins, the second of his wife. One showed Bruce with Pamela in what could only be described as an extremely compromising sexual position and the other, his wife in a similar position but with Samuel.

"Bloody hell, Liz. It's like the tomb of the pharaoh with the doodles and images. Looking at these, I reckon he manipulated each and every one of his victims. Do you think these two knew they were shagging one and the same or did they believe them to be two different people?"

Liz only raised her shoulders and then pointed to the boys. "The names under the pictures of Tony and Carl are those of the boys who betrayed him. Thomas, was the boy who supported him and continued to believe him, that's why he let Alan go not, as we believed, because we were closing in. Everything was planned, there's a timescale, a schedule. There appears to be a sequence, our man hasn't finished. This is just another part of his game. She looked at the photograph of Dr Brewster Smyth. He has unfinished business there."

"Look here!" Owen picked up a photograph that had fluttered from the wall, leaving only small pieces of Blu Tack as evidence of its exact position. They cornered the end of a drawn line from Pamela's photograph. Before handing it to Liz, Owen held it up, it was an image of John Melville with a younger man.

"That's Samuel. It was taken in the back garden." She looked back at the wall and placed it on the four Blu Tack blobs. Drawn on the wall and positioned directly above Melville's head, was a small, inked halo. "Angels and devils, Owen. Those who were kind and those who were not."

Get Forensics here and make sure Melville puts the dog next door. The key stays with us.

***

Dr Brewster Smyth refused to believe that his own son would in any way harm him, in fact, he refused to believe that his son could harm anyone, let alone kidnap and murder innocent kids.

"I'm a scientist not a police officer but believe me, you're attempting to arrest the wrong man. He's always been weak. Look, Chief Inspector, he couldn't even follow his own career path, he had to follow mine."

Cyril could not help but visualise him in his wife's underwear. "I don't believe he followed your lead totally."

Dr Smyth gave Cyril a look that would have intimidated many. "And you mean to imply?"

"Does he have your penchant for women's clothing and transvestites, Dr Smyth?"

"How the bloody hell do I know? You seem to have all the answers. I've noted, however, from the press, that still no villains have been caught for the murder of the two youngsters. How long's it been? Four or is it five weeks? All you can do is waste your time and mine discussing a life that I chose to live which quite frankly is neither against any law of this country nor any of your damn business. Now unless I'm under arrest for wearing the incorrect colour of lingerie, I should like to continue to run this business in peace."

"We have evidence to believe that your son has transformed himself into the two people comprising Samuel Dixon. Using that pretence, he has carried out the crimes as some type of revenge for events that occurred at the school. Samuel Dixon, Pamela Shepherd, if you prefer, was found dead this morning. All the evidence suggests murder. She has been dead for quite some time. At the moment we are unsure who kidnapped the children. Two other people have been found murdered and again evidence suggests that they were involved with the boys' deaths. On my way here, colleagues informed me that they have discovered photographs of all the murder victims. There was also an image of you."

Cyril held up his mobile. "This is the image."

Smyth took the phone. He laughed. "I'm portrayed as Satan, so much for my charity work!"

"Look, I can't force you to accept protection but I can offer you the strongest caution. If he is still actively seeking revenge you are in danger there is no question of that."

"I'll check under the bed every night, Chief Inspector, just to make sure the bogey men are not hiding. Now, as I've said before, I have work to do and so do you. Good day."

Cyril stood in the car park and phoned the station. Adrian Smyth had not been seen. His car was still at his apartment and both had been searched. A neighbour had observed him leaving the previous day with a large suitcase, a holiday abroad she had been told but she didn't know the destination. Blocks had been put on his passport and border agencies had been notified. If he had not already left, and according to the Border records he had not, then he was still free and travelling within the UK.

Cyril phoned Stuart Park. “Check all car hire firms in the area and see if either Smyth, Shepherd or Dixon has hired a vehicle in the last ten days. Check any matches with driving licence numbers and also look at railway bookings. If he's just hopped a train then there's nothing we can do.”

Chapter Thirty-Two

Preston train station was busy. Adrian Smyth walked up the slope from the platform, turning right over the bridge that crossed the lines before emerging onto Butler Street. He had visited the town before on many occasions as a youth but the most recent had been to attend a conference at the University. He turned up towards Fishergate, the main semi-pedestrianised street. The trundling case in tow was at this moment more of an inconvenience, but it was essential. He needed a coffee. He was on the last leg.

The Travelodge was both comfortable and innocuous. He had never stayed there before nor would he ever again. He gave a fake name and address, booking for three nights, paying cash and requesting a receipt. He neither wanted to waste further time nor effort. If the truth be known he had had enough.

The 280 bus service from Preston to Clitheroe was on time. Adrian Smyth chose a seat by the window and placed the small rucksack on the next seat. He looked around and counted six other passengers. The journey would take forty-five minutes. He glanced at the large complex that was Samlesbury aircraft works. An aircraft sat on a post at one of the gates but he took little interest.

Once in Clitheroe he found a taxi and gave an address. It would take fifteen minutes. Pendleton was as he remembered it, the brook babbled down the centre of the village set deep below the road. The pub was to the left, *The Swan with Two Necks.* The name had always amused him.

"Two necks means two heads means two personalities." He threw his rucksack over his shoulder and walked up the lane, stopping to look at an old stone bridge sitting away from the brook, preserved and safe. He could now see the house. It stood alone.

***

Cyril stared at the screen on one side of the incident room. The projected image showed the wall depicted as Owen and Liz had found it.

"Dead, dead, dead and dead. Then we have Pamela or Samuel, let's say Samuel, as officially she still is. We have a psychopathic motive for the deaths of the two boys and for the release of the other. I believe Samuel had to die for two reasons, firstly because he initially started this and secondly, he offered two perfect personalities with which to beguile and blackmail others into either supporting him in committing the crimes, or commit them for him. The defaced photograph Liz found downstairs would support this theory. Looking at the pattern of lines to photographs, we can see some aren't defaced but enhanced. They are set away as if they had nothing to do with anything other than, and I'm sorry to use the word, kindness. Melville and Gregson, although why he's even on the wall is a conundrum. The one person not here is...?"

Cyril waited.

"Mrs Hackworth."

"In one! Now why isn't she up on the wall of sinners if, as Dr Adrian Smyth pointed out, she was one of those who refused to believe and support him?"

"She did support him, she believed that he was telling the truth. According to the reports, she knew what had transpired and although she wasn't eager to see the police involved, she did protect the boy from expulsion. She brushed things under the carpet, moving him so that Dixon would have no further contact. She probably acted in a more sensitive and caring way than either his mother or certainly his father did."

"So why no photograph with a halo or a smiley face or anything else? Why is she missing?"

"Because she's somehow involved. There's no image of Dr Adrian Smyth either. Just thinking out loud." Owen's face reddened thinking he had made some totally ridiculous pronouncement.

Cyril looked at Liz. "What have we missed?"

***

The latch on the gate was as recalcitrant as he remembered and on the third tug it swung open. Lodge House was a traditional stone, detached country residence, once the home of the local GP. It stood slightly aloof of the village. It was the first home to have a separate building to house a car. The pathway leading to the front door was planted with lavender and Adrian let the aroma fill his nostrils as he deliberately brushed the bushes. He thought of Pamela, propped in the pantry and he smiled. Glancing at the large bay window he studied the figure sitting, watching his slow progress. They made eye contact. Adrian paused. Neither person waved nor smiled, they just stared.

Adrian kept his eyes on the elderly lady as long as he could. He then turned away following the path round to the rear of the house. He found what he was looking for, the side door to the garage was propped open using an old cobbler's last. He went inside.

Mrs Hackworth moved away from the window and checked that both the front and back doors were locked before picking up the phone.

***

The blue lights flashed along the grill of the unmarked police car. Owen drove whilst Cyril clung on in the passenger seat, his aviator sunglasses shielding his eyes from the low sunshine. Liz was in the back seat. Once through Blubberhouses, they climbed onto the moor heading for Bolton Bridge. Liz waited for the call from the Command Room. An earlier 999 call made from Mrs Hackworth's address had been taken at 17.43. A female was claiming that an intruder had entered outbuildings on her property. The local police were in attendance.

"Description of a male, about six foot with goatee beard. Can you believe it? Local police are communicating with her on her landline. She's moved upstairs on their advice and is now in one of the bedrooms. There has been no sighting of the intruder. As far as she's aware he's still in the outbuilding."

Cyril was beginning to feel a little sick, he began to yawn as sweat beaded his forehead and temples. He opened the window a fraction. The cool air helped.

"Shall I slow down, sir? You've turned a strange shade." Owen kept glancing across.

Liz interrupted Owen's attempt at a bedside manner. "Police are in position. What do you want them to do? Have them wait or go in?"

Cyril was still struggling to retain his lunch in his stomach.

"How long now, Owen?"

"Five minutes most."

"Have them hold position but maintain surveillance of the house entrances. If it looks as though our man is manoeuvring to enter, then tell them to move in."

The now narrow country lane leading to Pendleton was Cyril's idea of a nightmare. He clung on desperately not wanting to embarrass himself; the car window, now fully open, afforded him some respite. His shirt stuck to his body as streams of perspiration flowed down from his forehead. He marvelled at the way Liz managed to interact with a phone conversation and write notes throughout the rollercoaster journey.

Cyril breathed deeply, relieved to see the police vehicles positioned along the narrow lane. Owen pulled to one side and without a moment's notice, Cyril threw open the door allowing it to collide against a stone wall. He took three deep breaths.

"Go!"

Two plain-clothed officers moved down to meet them. They shook hands.

"Are you alright, sir, you're a strange colour?"

Cyril just smiled. "I'll be fine."

"He's in the garage area, the door's open. Mrs Hackworth is upstairs. We have visual. As you're SIO, sir, it's your call. We have four armed officers standing by at your command."

Cyril moved towards the rear of the property as directed by the two officers.

"You can see the door, it's propped open. There's been no movement since our arrival."

Cyril did not hesitate. "Send them in."

The dark-suited figures moved stealthily, communicating by the use of hand signals. One stood in front of the closed double doors as if expecting them to burst open. The other three made their way to the other door. Once in position they moved swiftly inside. Cyril heard their sharp, clear call.

"Armed police, armed..."

There was nothing further. After a moment one reappeared and moved his flat hand across his throat. No shots had been fired but it signalled that a body had been found. Cyril glanced across at Owen and Liz and then at the two officers. They moved along the path taken by the armed officers. Cyril was first through the door. Hanging from the wooden cross member that spanned the garage hung the body of Adrian Smyth. At his feet rested a small beard, removed by the contortions occurring during the hanging, and a set of overturned, wooden steps.

Even though there was no movement of air, the lifeless body turned slowly, suspended from the yellow and black nylon rope. The pattern did not escape Cyril's attention. Smyth had planned every last detail, even to the colour of the rope. He looked up at the face, the distended, bloodshot eyes stared at the workbench to his right.

Cyril moved over to it. A rucksack and a hard-backed notebook were neatly positioned; the book was open. A photograph filled the final page of the book. As if through habit, Cyril moved his hands behind his back so as not to touch anything. The grainy photograph was an image of Samuel Dixon and Adrian Smyth. Dixon had his arm around Smyth's shoulder. Smyth was dressed in girl's underwear. Only Dixon was smiling. Cyril removed his phone and captured the image. There was something about the background in the photograph that made his stomach churn. The rest of the book would have to remain a mystery until Forensics had analysed it.

Leaving the garage, he moved towards the front door of the house. Liz was sitting in what could be described as a drawing room with Mrs Hackworth; she was sipping tea. He glanced at the table and chair positioned in the bay window. Two glass tumblers sat on the table, one was half-filled with what looked like whisky, the other contained tablets of differing colours and sizes. Cyril picked up the liquid filled tumbler. He was right, a suicide kit.

"Mrs Hackworth, DCI Bennett. You met DS Graydon a couple of weeks ago. Do you mind if I take a look around your home?"

The elderly lady looked at Liz and then nodded. "Is something wrong? Is the man still in the garage?" Her voice sounded frail but false and almost lost within her frightened breath.

"Yes, he'll be there some time but I think you know that."

Cyril moved through the downstairs rooms before climbing the stairs. It was there that he found what he was looking for. He held his phone at the correct angle. The décor and the picture matched perfectly. The single bed to the right could just be seen. He returned downstairs.

Cyril collected the tumbler of tablets and placed it between Liz and the dejected Head teacher. He brought a chair placing it between Liz and Mrs Hackworth.

"Do you need reading glasses?" His voice seemed callous and hard. Liz turned to him, her expression quizzical.

Mrs Hackworth collected her glasses from the table by the window and returned to her seat. Cyril removed his phone and found the photograph before handing it to her. She handed it back. He passed it to Liz.

"Would you like to tell the Sergeant here where that was taken?"

The pause seemed to drag on for minutes.

"It was taken in the bedroom upstairs when Adrian was fourteen. I hope there are no others."

"Was Samuel Dixon your lover? I'm sure there will be photographs. Was he Pamela to you or Samuel?"

"It was a moment of weakness and then... I had my reputation and that of the school. You do anything, believe me, anything."

"Adrian Smyth was an innocent under your care... you're below contempt."

Cyril picked up the tumbler. "And these?"

"I tried, after the Sergeant here called a while back, I tried. Something told me that Samuel was dead. I knew that Adrian would come after I received the box, the tattoo equipment and the skin in the jar. I lied and he knew it. I really thought that he would make my end painful, that he would make me suffer but he didn't come to the door, he just stood and looked at me. It was a look I shall never forget. It was then that I realised that I had seen that look before, many years before. In that image you can see it. There was sadness in his eyes, a look of absolute betrayal and I knew then what was about to happen. He turned and went into the garage. I was too afraid to help. The way he looked at me from the pathway, I knew that it was time." She looked at the tablets. "How I tried, but I couldn't. I'm so sorry, Adrian, please forgive me." A tear rolled down her cheek and she wiped it away with the back of her hand. "Is he alive?"

Cyril stood. "Detective Sergeant Graydon will caution you and then you'll be arrested pending further enquiries. Dr Smyth has left a catalogue of evidence in the garage as a full and final chapter in his difficult and confused life. Whether we will ever fully understand how those selfish, abusive crimes you committed against that boy affected his mind is not for us to determine, we can only interpret the evidence and follow the exact letter of the law."

He moved out of the house. He needed air. Removing his e-cigarette he inhaled deeply. The menthol infusion filled his mouth taking away the bitter taste.

The SOCO team had already arrived and the medical team was moving towards the garage. All it had taken was one bizarre summer and someone's life had been totally destroyed. Cyril collected Liz and Owen, thanked the officers and moved to the car.

"Passenger seat, Owen. It's a steady run back."

Liz grabbed Owen's arm. "We don't know what time we'll finish tonight but ask me if I'd like a drink after work!"

Owen blushed slightly recalling their conversation. "Would you like a drink after work if the pubs are still open?"

"Love one."

"And if the pubs are closed, I have beer at my place." She winked and smiled.

Owen continued to blush.

"Are you two coming or staying?"

Chapter Thirty-Three

The music was low. Cyril sat with his feet on the coffee table, looking through the photocopied pages of Adrian Smyth's diary. It had detailed his time in school and his abuse at the hands of Dixon and his Head teacher. It detailed his father's departure from the family home and his university life. There was never any mention of friends, neither girls nor boys in his life. He possessed no real memories of friends, only enemies. It was a chronological history of his life until he kidnapped Pamela, detailing how he had kept her locked away and how he had taken her place looking after her aunt. He had robbed her of her personality, had invaded every part of her life. He discovered the house in Hampsthwaite, her relationship with Gregson, he got to know the people she knew, the Jenkins and how he quickly took over their lives too.

At one point the pages in the diary were divided down the middle with a thick red line. From one person grew two and the diary took the form of those two people who grew in his psyche. Pamela and Samuel both became real, each had a separate story to tell in graphic detail. Photographs supported the written word. The kidnappings and the murders, the purification, the mollification, were all described by Samuel in minute detail, how the process would help others in the long term, how it would make the bitter sweet. It all seemed as confused as his mind. What did prove fascinating was that Pamela's account contained no mention of the kidnappings or the killings; it detailed Liz's meetings and happy times with Bruce Jenkins, of how kind he had been. It also mentioned John Melville and his support and bizarrely the love she felt for the aunt. If ever there was a Janus figure where one grew into two so disparate people then this was it. On three occasions, a full page reverted to the life of Dr Adrian Smyth. It was as if nothing in the pages before mattered, it was just his account of daily life.

Cyril turned to the last page. In the centre, written boldly and in the same script and by the same hand, according to the Forensic analysts, as that found on the jar labels, were the words:

You think that I died today, you are wrong, as from today I am now free.
But what of you, those who abused me, what of you?
You will carry the guilt of these crimes until eternity, you and Samuel and Pamela
And for me?

I AM THE MASTER OF MY FATE;
I AM THE CAPTAIN OF MY SOUL

INVICTUS.

Cyril put down the sheets, he had seen enough. It should have been up to the psychologists to determine whether or not he was of sound mind, but a rope, the colour of a bee's back had solved that dilemma. There was now only one person standing trial and that was for historical child abuse. He opened a bottle of Black Sheep beer and collected his electronic cigarette before moving to the window. The streetlight flickered, first pink and then slowly turning orange before casting a warm glow along the road. He turned to look at the sheets of paper spread haphazardly on the table and wondered why Hackworth had been spared, why she was not the first one to suffer; there would always be unanswered questions. He drank the last of the beer and in doing so closed his mind to the case.

Chapter Thirty-Four

The overcast autumn sky seemed heavy. A light wisp of morning mist clung to the river's slow-moving surface like a white chiffon scarf; the leaves on the overhanging trees, flanking the river's twisting banks, were just showing signs of turning to their deep, autumnal russet. Occasionally a leaf would fall before drifting towards the water. Cyril stood in the small lay-by, leaning against his car. He slowly inhaled the menthol vapour from his electronic cigarette. His eyes followed the mist as it formed a variety of shapes before it tucked under the narrow road bridge. The exhaled vapour that drifted lazily from his nostrils only added to the ethereal grey of the morning.

His thoughts focused on Tony and Carl. A tear crept from his left eye, more in frustration and anger than from sadness. The answers had been staring them in the face all along and he had repeatedly kicked himself for not spotting the clues earlier. He knew, however, that at times like these he had to place everything into perspective or the doubts, the frustrations and the feeling of total inadequacy would squash him, along with his natural ability and his self-confidence. He had to convince himself that he had done everything that he could with the evidence before him. He did not have a crystal ball, he could not see what was not there. But the deaths of the two boys hung heavily on his shoulders. The freeing of the third child had meant nothing when he viewed his overall performance, after all, that was part of the murderer's plan.

He thought of Dr Adrian Smyth; to all intents and purposes he was a successful man with talent and skills, but all would prove meaningless, destroyed by the devious acts, by the closely-knit secrets adults weave to protect themselves and to frighten the young into submission, often ignorant of the devastating, emotional trauma they spawn. The truth was that eventually, at some point, you would reap what you sow. Cyril felt a degree of sadness for the man.

All of those Latin statements flashed in his head. He took a coin from his pocket and without looking at it, tossed it through the misty veil and into the water. It was something he had read about. When Roman soldiers crossed water they would often toss a coin to the river god, a votive gift, believing that it would make their onward journey more comfortable and safer. He needed to subscribe to that too.

"It's done, Cyril. It took a while but you won. Against all the odds your team was successful," he said out loud. A vehicle passed. He slipped his e-cigarette into his pocket and got into the car.

Ilkley was busy for a Tuesday. He turned down Little Lane before driving up Nelson Road. He thought of Liz and then an image emerged of the slumped, neatly-wrapped body of Pamela Shepherd, but he quickly put the thought from his mind. The auction house he had come to visit was on his right.

He entered and smiled at the receptionist. She coloured a little and returned his smile. The viewing and auction rooms were at the top of the stairs. He could hear the auctioneer's Irish accent echo within the old hall. It was busy, all the seats were taken and people stood around the room. The area of paintings was closed until the morning sale had been completed, then he would be able to inspect the painting he hoped to buy. It was then that the auctioneer's voice made his heart jump as he announced the sale of a jewelled bee-styled brooch. Would he always think of this case every time he saw a jar of honey or a bee?

The painting he had come to buy was only small, a work by William Ralph Turner, a Cheshire artist. It was in oil depicting a Salford church. The figures in the painting were rather indistinct, true to the artist's style, but they had fascinated Cyril when he saw it in the catalogue. He was sure the artist had depicted Lowry tipping his hat to a passer-by. It was lot 312.

Cyril waited patiently and his heart rate increased as his lot approached. All thoughts of the last weeks slowly evaporated, he was now fully focused on the auctioneer's swift, no nonsense approach. It was then his turn.

"Lot 312, William Ralph Turner oil. I have several commission bids on the books and two telephone lines. I can start the bidding at..."

For the second time, within an hour, Cyril's heart sank.

"Stercus accidit..." he said quietly to himself... "Stercus accidit. But why me?"

It was then that he realised, he only had the Roman God to blame.

He smiled to himself, looked up and swiftly left the saleroom.

Featured Artist

In this novel, Cyril hopes to bid on a painting at auction entitled, '*Salford Church*' by the Manchester artist, William Ralph Turner. In all my books I like to highlight a little about one of the pieces of artwork mentioned. In each case I either own or have owned the specific work.

William Ralph Turner
(1920-2013)

William Ralph Turner was a self-taught artist who produced a large quantity of work, much of which concentrated on the industrial north. He painted scenes from around the north west. As a keen cyclist there are many scenes depicting his cycle tours.

Turner was rediscovered in 2000 when he was eighty years of age by David Gunning, an art dealer from Todmorden.

Parkinson's disease forced Turner to stop painting in 2005. He was given a retrospective at *Gallery Oldham.*

Acknowledgements

Debbie

What a star you are. Thank You X

Carrie

Thank you so much for your continued patience and support.

Dr Richard Barrett

For inspirational conversations, thank you.

Kat McCooey-Heap

Thank you.

Dan O'Brien

Cover photograph – photolincs.co.uk

Poems that inspired, with my grateful thanks

Charles Hamilton Musgrove(1871-1926)

'The Dungeoned Anarchist'

William Ernest Henley (1849–1903)

'Invictus'

Printed in Great Britain
by Amazon